The Commodore's Barge Is Alongside

MAX BRAITHWAITE

The Commodore's Barge Is Alongside

McClelland and Stewart

Copyright© 1979 by Max Braithwaite

Reprinted 1982

ISBN: 0-7710-1633-6

The Canadian Publishers
McClelland and Stewart Limited
25 Hollinger Road
Toronto, Ontario M4B 3G2

Printed and bound in Canada by Webcom Ltd.

This is a work of fiction. Any resemblance
to persons living or dead is coincidental.

Canadian Cataloguing in Publication Data

Braithwaite, Max, 1911-
The commodore's barge is alongside

ISBN 0-7710-1633-6

I. Title.

PS8503.R34C64   C813'.5'4   C79-094063-9
PR9199.3.B735C64

To George Hood and all
the other ratings of the RCNVR.

1

The Porpoise
That Couldn't Swim

To say that the War – that's the big war of 1939-45, not the numerous little ones they've had since – changed the lives of an entire generation is a cliché, but like a good many other clichés it happens to be true.

Now, looking back on it some forty years later, I realize that it changed my life beyond recall. On that fateful Sunday morning of September 3, 1939, when I crawled out of bed at four o'clock in the morning to listen on the radio to that sad declaration of Neville Chamberlain, I was living in the small city of Wabagoon in the middle of the Canadian prairies. I had been out of high school for two years and, except for my paper route, had never had a steady job in my life. I was a member of that "great army of unemployed," a useless appendage on the body economic, a bum.

The worst kind of bum, really, because I was bumming off my parents who, with Dad unemployed for two years, could barely afford to support themselves and my brother and sister. Lord knows I'd tried hard enough to get a job. I'd even travelled by freight as far as Vancouver looking for work on the boats and to Flin Flon looking for work in the mines. No dice. From all that, I and the rest of my generation were rescued by that madman Adolf Hitler.

I remember vividly how Dad got the whole family up in the middle of the night so that we could hear the actual words of the British Prime Minister, a great thrill in those early days of radio. We huddled around the old gothic-shaped Philco in the livingroom of our house on Duke Street: Dad in his pyjamas with the ragged string hanging down over his pot belly, Ma in her scruffy dressing gown curled up in the old black leather chair, Doug and Mary lying on the rug.

When Chamberlain finished with the words "and consequently this country is at war with Germany," Dad viciously turned the knob of the radio to Off.

"I knew it!" and then he swore, which was unusual for him, and Ma didn't protest, which was unusual for her. "The bloody fools have done it again!"

Mary uncurled her gangly legs and said, "I think war is nuts!" and went back to bed.

Ma said nothing, but her tired face was a little more creased than usual as she got up and walked wearily towards the stairs.

Doug leaped to his feet. "Are you going to go, Dink?" he shouted.

"Not on your life."

And I meant it. All through high school our pacifist-minded teachers had convinced us that war was evil and that if nobody went there would be no more wars. The world was finished with war, we were told over and over again. In our debating clubs we proved that "The Treaty of Versailles was the most unjust document ever signed by nations of the first rank," that wars were arranged for profit by "robber barons," and that total disarmament was the way of the future. All the time ignoring the fact that Nazi Germany was building the mightiest war machine in modern history. Was ever a generation so naïve?

The day following Chamberlain's speech, no less a voice than that of King George VI was heard direct from Buckingham Palace warning us that "The task will be hard," and "There may be dark days ahead," thereby putting the official stamp on the war to come. We were for it.

But no dark days came. In fact, for quite a while, apart from the sinking of some ships, nothing happened. We talked of the phony war and were somewhat disappointed that all the flag-waving seemed to be for naught. Then in the spring of 1940 all hell broke loose, and within a few short weeks France and Belgium and Norway had been occupied and Britain stood alone, facing her greatest danger since 1066.

By that time we'd all become gung-ho for war. The flag-waving and the speech-making had been too much for us. Besides, enlistment for many meant the first good overcoat in years, not to mention dental work and a release from the terrible boredom of the Depression.

So it happened that on the second day of July, a hot, dusty day, which is to say a typical summer day on the prairies, I put on my blue serge suit, applied elbow grease and polish to my shabby black oxfords, vaselined my unruly blond hair into a gooey pompadour and, with as much bravado as I could muster, marched down Ridgeway Street, across the bridge over the wide Wabagoon River, down Regal Avenue to the corner of Queen Street, where His Majesty's Canadian Ship *Porpoise* lay at anchor in a patch of weeds, and went aboard.

HMCS *Porpoise*! Was there ever in the history of naval warfare a more scruffy ship?

The war had caught everybody unprepared, and Canada's fledgling navy most of all. Suddenly the service was required to recruit and train men for the hundreds of corvettes and other small fighting craft feverishly being built. This meant dragging youngsters from the city streets, farms, and small towns, and in a matter of weeks making sailors of them. Most of us on the prairies had never seen a body of water larger than a slough or been aboard a floating craft larger than a raft. To accomplish its task, the navy established training divisions in all of the major cities and called them "ships." They ranged in size from HMCS *York*, the automotive building in Toronto's CNE grounds, to HMCS *Porpoise*.

The only available building in Wabagoon was a one-storey brick garage, long abandoned and falling apart. Suddenly, like the men who were to man her, she was given a new lease on life and elevated to the eminence of junior partner in the world's mightiest and proudest service, The Royal Navy.

She wasn't even close to the Wabagoon River, which wound like a great muddy snake through the centre of the city. Rather she was across the street from a spur of the Canadian National Railway, with the usual things found along such a track: a grocery warehouse, a farm implement company headquarters, some coal shacks, and a lot of weeds.

The front – oops – *bow* of the ship extended about one hundred and fifty feet along Regal Avenue and the starboard side about three hundred feet along Queen Street. On the port side was a vacant lot full of pigweed through which peeked rusty bits of fender, old engine blocks, tires and other junk that accumulates around old garages. The stern faced on a back alley.

The port side of the ship, extending from the big garage doors in the bow to the C.P.O.'s office in the stern, was the parade deck. The starboard side of the bow consisted of offices and officers' wardroom. This latter had been the garage's showroom in other days and boasted a hardwood floor and huge draped windows that faced both Regal Avenue and Queen Street. The remainder of the garage, with its floor of bumpy concrete and its grease-splattered brick walls, had been scrubbed and polished to give it some semblance of nautical grandeur.

So here I was, joining the navy.

As I walked through that front door (pardon me, went aboard), my thoughts were a jumble of things nautical. All the nice girls love a sailor; a girl in every port; sailing sailing, over the bounding main. From years of reading about pirate ships and First World War stories and seeing dozens of movies, I knew what sailors were all right, and what was expected of them. I also knew that I would rather enlist in the navy than be drafted into the army where, it was well understood, people got shot.

I found myself in a large room filled with desks and filing cabinets, with three small offices partitioned off along the sides which, I later learned, were inhabited by the captain, the paymaster, and the recruiting officer. The main room was full of officious-looking young men dressed in natty blue uniforms and wearing peaked caps, either sitting at desks or rushing about with papers in their hands. Naturally, since I knew that ordinary seamen wore jumpers, bell bottom trousers, and flat peakless caps, I took these to be officers.

I approached the nearest one and made my first of many snafus by saluting him smartly. He looked at me blankly.

"What the hell is that for?" he asked.

"I want to enlist, sir."

"I'm not a sir. I'm a writer. You want Donner. That desk over there."

I went over and stood in front of a desk where another writer was banging away on an ancient Remington upright. He stopped, ripped the page out of the machine, ran another in, and without looking at me barked, "Yeah?"

"I want to enlist."

"Last name?"

"Diespecker."

He glanced up at me as though to say, What in hell kind of name is that? and I went on the defensive. But worse was to come.

"First name, or names?"

"Robin."

"As in redbreast?"

I nodded.

"Other names?"

Well, I might as well. "Evelyn Francis."

He didn't look up this time, but kept on typing without batting an eye.

Those damned names of mine. I think that, allowing for the awfulness of the others, Diespecker was the worst. There are so many things that dirty-minded kids can do with a name like that. Bruce Sharnon called me Leastpecker until I punched him out, but that was one of the least opprobrious derivations.

A name like that can do terrible things to a kid. Imagine standing up beside your seat on the first day of school and announcing to the world that your name is Robin Evelyn Francis Diespecker. The only thing I could do about the laughter that swelled from every side of the room was join it. Which may account for the clownish twist to my nature which I'm sure was at least partly responsible for the trouble I got into aboard *Porpoise*.

My name affected my personality in another way. You can't back away from such a handle. Like a hockey player who is speared or elbowed or high-sticked, when taunted with your name you must retaliate or be forever branded as a poltroon. So I became a scrapper. The smallest hint of a gibe on my name and I'd pile in and either beat up the offender or get beaten up. This proclivity to fisticuffs also helped foul up my naval career. Clowning and pugnaciousness are two qualities not greatly appreciated by the hard-headed leading seamen and petty officers who were to become masters of my fate.

I didn't tell Donner that my nickname was Dink. This had been donated to me early on by the kids in school. I didn't care much for it, but it sure beat the three my mother had inflicted on me, and so, to everyone but my parents, my teachers, and certain girl friends, I'd become Dink Diespecker.

Donner's next questions were routine.

"Age?"

"Twenty."

"Education?"

"Senior matric."

"Got your diploma?"

"Yes. Here it is."

"Hmm . . . nineteen thirty-eight . . . honours. Okay. Nationality?"

"Canadian."

"No such thing. What was your father?"

"Canadian."

"Where did your folks come from originally?"

"From their folks, I guess."

"Never mind that. What's your racial origin?"

"I'm not sure. Quite a mixture. Why not just put down Anglo Saxon?"

12

And so it went. He found out I'd been born in Wabagoon and lived there all my life, that my parents were both living, that I had two siblings, both living, that I went to the United Church and that if I got into the navy I could live at home since there were no messing facilities aboard *Porpoise*.

He ripped the form out of the typewriter, handed it to me, and said, "Over there," indicating a worn bench along a wall beside a door, where two other civilians sat in worried silence.

I sat down beside a big fellow of about my age with a ragged haircut and a faded work shirt, baggy pants and boots with brown stains around the soles. Cow manure if I'd ever smelled it. He shifted over on the bench to make room, and muttered, "Hello."

"Hi. Nice day for it anyway."

On the prairies a sure conversation opener is always the weather, for the weather is always uncertain and determines absolutely the economic status of all those who live off the land and of those who live off the people who live off the land.

"Could use rain, though," he said, confirming, along with the smell of the boots and big rough hands, my first impression that he was a farm boy.

"Where you from?" I asked.

"Wannego. Ever been there?"

"No."

"What you going in for?"

"What?"

"I mean what branch?"

"Haven't thought of it. Just want to be a sailor and get to sea."

"Stoker's the best," the man sitting next to him stated flatly. He was smaller, better dressed, and looked as though he'd been around some.

We both looked at him, me leaning forward to see past my neighbour.

"Why do you say that?" I asked.

"Friend of mine, he told me. Been in the reserves. Stokers got it made. Used to shovel coal but now they just turn taps and watch gauges. Got it made."

"But don't you have to spend your time, like, down in the - " farm boy began.

"Down below?" town boy prompted. "Yeah, sure, but that's the best place to be when the bullets start to fly. Up on deck you're a sitting duck."

Farm boy shook his head with a frown. "I don't know. Hate like hell to be closed in like that. What if the ship gets hit or something? How would you get out?"

Town boy laughed. "If she takes a fish amidships, you're a gonner wherever you are. No, it's the boiler room for me."

"My name's Sam," farm boy said. "Sam Waldress. What's yours?"

"Mike," town boy replied. "Mike Jones."

Gawd, it must be nice to have names like Sam and Mike. They were both looking at me and I knew I was in for it.

"Dink," I said. "My first name's so awful . . ."

"Dink? Jees, what a handle." And then noticing the belligerent look on my face. "But not bad. Yeah, Dink. Glad to know you, Dink."

We shook hands all around awkwardly. From somewhere beyond the flimsy partitions came the hollow sound of heavy boots on cement floor, many heavy boots. And then a high voice. "Halt." The footsteps stopped abruptly. Then the voice again. "Jee-sus kee-ryst. I mean gawd-amighty! Youse guys. You march like a bunch of farmers!"

Sam winced.

"I told ya. Pick em up and put em down smartly, and swing yer arms high. Elbows straight, hands loosely clenched." It was a singsong now. "Keeping in step with the man next to you at all times." Then the disgust again. "Some of youse guys honest-to-gawd don't know yer right foot from yer left! This is yer right. This is yer left. Memorize that." Then tiredly, "Okay, stan at ease. Stan easy!"

This was followed by a rush of feet and a cheery jabber of voices.

"Sounds like a real tough killick," Mike whispered happily.

Sam's forehead wrinkled in the frown I was soon to know so well. "What's a killick?" he asked.

Mike regarded him with the scorn of the enlightened. "Jees! Leading seaman. Do most of the drilling and teaching of the new entries. Friend in the reserves, he told me all about it. Boy, the navy." Mike's square face beamed. "That's the service!"

A harried civilian emerged from the recruiting office and a bored voice from within shouted, "Okay, Donner, next man."

"Yes, sir!" Donner looked at us. "Jones, you're next. Right in there." Mike disappeared through the door and the murmur of voices began again. We went on waiting. Fighting the Hun, I was to learn in the months ahead, consisted mostly in waiting somewhere to hear your name called.

Sam squirmed uneasily, knowing he'd be called soon. "I never done anything like this before," he said. "Ain't been in the city more'n a couple a times."

"Nothing to it," I said uncertainly. "Just like any interview in high school."

"Never been to high school. Quit in Grade Six when they closed the school because nobody could pay no taxes."

"What have you been doing since?"

"Working at home on the farm. Gosh all crop to take off these last years, though."

We sat in silence. Then Mike came out with a big grin on his face. "I'm in."

"Great."

"Over here, Jones," Donner barked, and with a broad, happy smile Mike left us.

Sam went in through the door like a kid going into the principal's office. I watched Donner type and answer the phone and wondered what it would be like to be a "writer." No, I didn't want that.

Sam finally came out, looking completely bewildered, shaking his head and muttering the word "cook." Donner directed him towards the next step of the process.

15

Now it was my turn. A pudgy man of about fifty was sitting at a desk. He wore a blue uniform with two gold wavy stripes with a circle above on each sleeve. His shirt was white, his collar stiffly starched and his tie black. He looked up at me and said, "Sit down . . . Dies . . . Dies . . . Diespecker? Is that your name?"

"Yes, sir. I'm afraid it is."

"Robin Evelyn Francis Diespecker?"

"Yes, sir. I'm usually called Dink."

"Well, as the bard said, what's in a name? A dink by any other name would still stink." He chuckled to himself, obviously making a mental note to repeat this rouser in the wardroom.

He gave me what I'm sure he considered to be his sharp, penetrating look. "Why do you want to join the navy, Diespecker?"

"Well . . ." I'm always floored by damned fool questions.

"Consider it safer than the army, eh?"

"Is it?"

He looked up sharply and I'd swear he was going to say, as in a cops and robbers movie, "I ask the questions here, wise guy!" But he refrained and just grunted.

"So, Diespecker. I see you passed your senior matric in June of 1938. What have you been doing in the two years since then?"

"Nothing. Unemployed."

"You mean you couldn't get a job? The Depression was over by then, surely?"

"Maybe down east, but not out here. It was worse than ever."

"How did you put in your time?"

"Well, for one thing I tried to get into the naval reserves. You see I've always been fascinated by the sea. Read all the stories I could get my hands on. And the poems we had in high school. Like those of John Masefield."

"Oh yes, 'Give me a tall ship and a star to steer her by.' Why couldn't you get into the reserves?"

"I was on the list, but they weren't taking any more guys. I hung around the barracks some."

"What else did you do?"

"Well, I went harvesting. But there wasn't much crop to harvest. Delivered leaflets. Tried selling encyclopaedias door to door, but couldn't do it. Nobody had any money. Stuff like that."

"But you didn't try to join the army?"

"No, I guess I was kind of hooked on the navy. I was waiting for this place to open."

"All right. Tell me what you can do that might be of some use to the navy."

"I don't know. But I could be trained to do something."

"Can you sail a boat?"

"No."

"Ever have any military training?"

"Just in cadets in school."

"Officer, sergeant, corporal?"

"Private."

"I see."

I thought it might be time for a little levity. "The drill teacher tried to make me a corporal once, but I turned the platoon right instead of left and marched them down a twenty-foot embankment."

He just looked at me.

"Don't suppose you've ever been in a boat, out here on these godforsaken, drought-ridden prairies."

"Just a rowboat once at camp."

He brightened. "Scout camp?"

"No. Trail Rangers."

"Never heard of them. Can you cook?"

"No."

"How do you know? We could teach you. We have openings for cooks."

"I don't think I could ever learn to cook, sir. I'd rather be a seaman."

He sighed heavily and shoved some papers around on his desk. "You're in luck, Diespecker. Just so happens we've had a signal from headquarters to take on twenty seamen. Although I don't know how they're going to make seamen out of you plough jockeys."

17

"Where are you from, sir?" I ventured to ask.

"Me? Nova Scotia. Been around boats and ships all my life. Why in the last war . . . but no matter, no matter." He became all business. "Okay, Diespecker. We'll try to make a seaman out of you. Cannon fodder, cannon fodder. That is, if you pass the medical."

So I went where Donner directed me, down a corridor and into the sick bay. Mike and Sam were already there, sitting on a bench stark naked, clutching pieces of paper and shivering. Mike jerked his eyes towards the closed door of the inner office and whispered huskily, "Know what that joker tried to make me? A cook! No chance!"

"What did you tell him?" I whispered back.

"Up yours! That's what I'd like to of told him."

"Are you going to be a stoker?"

"Damned right, or it's aye-woll for me."

"What?"

"Aye-woll. Over the hill. Split. Take it on the lam."

"Oh sure."

We were interrupted by a sick bay tiffy in a white coat and glasses who stuck his head out the door, pointed a bony finger at me and snarled, "You. Get those clothes off."

I did.

Sam was still looking bewildered, and terribly embarrassed. I don't think he'd ever bared himself in front of another before, not having the advantage of a YMCA swimming pool. I looked the other way and was careful not to let my eyes go in his direction throughout our conversation.

"How about you?" Mike asked Sam.

"I don't know. Gosh, I never cooked anything in my life. How can he say I'd make a perfect cook?"

Mike whispered a snicker. "You've been diddled, Sammy me boy."

The tiffy stuck his head out again. "Okay, you're next." Mike winked at us and swaggered through the door, pendulum swinging jauntily.

"So you're going to be a cook," I said to Sam.

"Gosh help the guys who got to eat it." "Gosh," I was gradually to discover, was the strongest expletive in Sam's vocabulary. He sat there on the cold bench, hunched over his nakedness, one big paw covering his genitals, and brooded over his fate. Then he brightened. "Ever hear the joke about the three hunters and them cooking?"

If I'd known Sam then as I later got to know him, I'd have quickly said I knew the story, for Sam, like many another prairie farm boy, was an irrepressible story-teller. Frowning seriously, he began his recitation, never stopping for breath.

"Well, there was these three guys went hunting, see, on a week's trip it was and they decided that they'd draw straws to see who'd be cook see and then that guy would cook until somebody complained about the cooking and then he'd have to take over the job. Well, the guy who drew the cook job made a couple of good meals and then he saw that he was going to be the cook for the whole week if he didn't get somebody to complain, so he made some awful meals. Man, they were terrible, but still nobody complained. Well, finally he got desperate and went out and got a cow flap and heated it up in the oven, you know a cow flap, and served it with salt and pepper and ketchup and everything for dinner that night. Well, the guys were hungry after being out all day and the first guy took a big bite of it and started to chew and then his face went white. 'Gosh almighty,' he said, 'that tastes like cow manure!' And then real quick he added, 'But good!' "

I guffawed lustily, but the hollowness of it in those sterile surroundings stopped me and I grinned my appreciation.

Mike came out and hurried off to his next assignment. Sam had his turn, and then the tiffy stuck his head out again. "Okay." He consulted his sheet and actually grinned. "Diespecker. Yer next."

I followed him through the door into an anteroom just wide enough for his small desk and a straight-backed chair.

The tiffy ran a long sheet of paper into his typewriter and started barking questions at me. After the usual name, address, place of birth, age, education, he rattled off some new ones. "Ever have measles, mumps, chickenpox, tuberculosis, jaundice, VD, kidney trouble, fainting spells?" I tried to tell him about the fainting spell I had in Grade Six when I was standing at the blackboard in ninety-five-degree heat trying to figure out the complexities of decimals, but he didn't listen. On went the list and to some I answered yes and some no. Then he ripped out the sheet, handed it to me and barked, "In there."

Inside the next door was the doctor's office, with all the usual paraphernalia and a nice man. He was tall, well over six feet, and held himself with a slightly bent position as though to compensate for his height. His head was big and slightly bald, and he had a wide, friendly face that smiled a lot. He was in his shirt sleeves and sweating slightly. He looked like, and in fact had been, a family doctor from one of the prairie towns, used to dealing with farmers and small-town people.

"Hi," he said. "Sit down." He looked at my form. "Diespecker. Robin Evelyn Francis Diespecker." Pursed his lip. "Bet you've licked a few guys over that one!" His tone was friendly and I didn't bristle. "Wait until I tell you my name. Coffin. Imagine a doctor named Coffin. Should have either changed my name or my profession years ago." I grinned my appreciation. "That's not the worst of it, either. My first name is Hyram and so I get Hy. Hy Coffin. Everybody here just calls me Doc."

Doc was "okay." I was soon to learn that everybody who came into contact with him designated him so. From a rating's standpoint there are two kinds of officers, and only two—"prick" and "okay." Doc was okay.

Doc prodded, poked, and listened, peered into my various orifices, told me to come around some time and a tiffy would syringe the wax out of my left ear, said, "Wish to hell I were in as good shape as you," and said he'd be seeing me around.

That afternoon I went back to the recruiting officer and was sworn in. I was in the navy. My Gawd, in the navy! Wowee!

2

Stone Frigate

"This is a ship, and don't any of you ever forget it."

We were standing in front of Chief Petty Officer Lightson, who was as stiff as a ramrod and just about as soft. More, much more, about him later.

A lot of things had happened in the past two days, all of them exciting. But most exciting of all was the drawing and marking of our uniforms and gear. Ah, that uniform, how I loved it, and, as a matter of fact, still do. Not just because it was the first new clothes I'd had in years, but from the round flat white cap to the sturdy black boots it was a wow. "Round rig" it was called (as opposed to the "fore-and-aft rig" worn by petty officers, writers, sick bay tiffies, *et al*) and whoever designed it surely knew something about how to make a man feel sexy.

The jumper, now. Blue wool and form fitting (the first act of every new entry was to take his jumper to a tailor and have it made so skin tight it required a zipper down the side) topped with the large braid-trimmed collar, the lanyard knotted just so, and the white jersey showing at the chest. The bell bottom trousers, plenty of cloth, none of your narrow sissy pants of the airforce or the sloppy ones of the army. Not to mention the heavy blue overcoat and the pea jacket and the working fatigues and all the rest. I loved 'em all.

But I didn't love Chief Petty Officer Lightson. I can see him now, tall, lean, sharp-faced and handsome. His uniform fitted perfectly, trousers always pressed, shoes always shined, collar always crisp and clean. He was a model of how a navy man should look. Chest out, stomach in, hands at the sides with fingers slightly curled. He stood straight, sat straight and thought straight.

He was on loan from the Royal Navy, and it seemed to me that he hated being ashore, hated Canada, and especially the cold, wind-swept prairies; hated *Porpoise* and the fresh-faced young officers who had never been to sea, and ratings he had to, in the short space of six weeks, "whip into shape."

Why? Perhaps because he just couldn't understand the free-and-easy, undisciplined, un-military, skeptical attitude of prairie youth. The older of us, especially (most recruits were barely seventeen), who'd had our noses rubbed in life by the Depression, tended to believe in little and hold nothing sacred. To Lightson, on the other hand, the navy was sacred, as was proper respect for your betters, especially those in uniform. And he was determined that before we left *Porpoise* we'd believe as he did and have the proper "attitude." To Lightson, attitude was all.

"His Majesty's Canadian Ship *Porpoise*," Lightson barked. "And she's a tight ship. And you are the men who will keep her tight. Over there is the quarterdeck where you go ashore and come aboard. If I ever hear a man say he's going out or coming in, I'll see to it he never does it again. Oh yes I will. Understood?"

We nodded our heads to indicate it was, and Mike, the damned fool, shouted out, "Aye aye, sir."

"Who said that?"

"I did, sir." Mike didn't sound so cocky now.

"Take one step forward."

Mike stepped forward.

"What's your name?" Lightson's sharp nose was quivering like a setter's at point.

"Mike, sir."

"Last name?"

"Jones, sir."

"Jones. That figures. Well, Mike Jones, what is my rank?"

"You're the Chief, sir." Then proudly, "Chief Petty Officer."

"You lie, Jones. You lie in your teeth. That is not my rank. I do not have a rank. Only commissioned officers have rank." The eyes flashed with something I didn't quite get at first and then I did – contempt. "And only commissioned officers are addressed as sir. Not non-commissioned officers. Not leading seamen, not instructors, not petty officers, not chief petty officers. Understand that?"

"Yes, sir. I mean, yes."

"What else?"

Poor Mike was floored. He searched his brain for what Lightson might mean. "Admirals?"

This brought a burst of laughter from the platoon and a sweet smile to the mouth of Chief Petty Officer Lightson.

"Admirals," he said gently. "Admirals. I don't mean that, you numskull. What else must you remember about non-commissioned officers and commissioned officers?"

Mike was beat. A hand shot up in the ranks. It belonged to Brown-nose Stickley. His mother never gave him that name, but the ratings soon did. That or "Suckhole" or "Bumboy" or "Kissass," take your pick.

"Okay, Stickley?"

"You don't salute a non-commissioned officer or a leading hand. Just commissioned officers."

"Keeerect. And with the navy salute. Not that abortion of an army salute or an air force salute, but a navy salute. You'll be instructed in that salute this afternoon. Jones, get back in your place and report to my office at Stand Easy."

He went on instructing us in the parts of HMCS *Porpoise*. Upper deck, lower deck, poop deck. "There are no floors aboard ship, you understand, but decks. No walls, but bulkheads, no stairways, but companionways, no front, but a bow, no rear, but a stern," and on and on until looking

23

through the big open garage door in the bow I expected to see not hot, dusty Regal Avenue with the bread wagon peacefully clopping past and the railway beyond, but the bounding main with twenty subs coming up on our starboard quarter.

Finally the bosun piped Stand Easy and, after being dismissed by Lightson, we all rushed for the canteen.

This was in a corner made by a rough partition that separated the main part of the ship from a big room in the stern which had a wooden floor and was used for instructional and recreational purposes. The canteen was stocked with cigarettes, tobacco, chocolate bars, soft drinks, and various other sundries that might take a rating's fancy. It was operated solely and entirely by Lightson, who possessed the only key. Later I learned that ships' canteens were operated by canteen committees with the profits, which were high, used to purchase amenities for the crew – a piano or a juke box or whatever. But aboard *Porpoise* in those early war days Lightson ran the whole show and kept the profits.

Sam and I got ourselves a coke and a chocolate bar and sat down to shoot the breeze. We had a lot of catching up to do. Sam had found himself a boarding house and when he gave me the address I winced.

"What are the people like?" I asked.

"Nice. Real nice. Mrs. Knox said she didn't usually take boarders."

"But because you are such a fine-looking lad she'd make an exception."

"Yeah. How did you know?"

"Just guessed. How about Mr. Knox?"

"He's away just now. Just Mrs. Knox and Gertie and Marjorie and Bert is all I saw."

"Which one do you sleep with?"

"Bert. But not for long. Marjorie is leaving. Going to join the WAACs, I think. Then I can have her room."

"What about Gertie?"

"What about her?" So help me, Sam was blushing.

"Well, you know. What's she like?"

"She's swell."

24

I took a closer look at him. In his uniform he looked entirely different from the farm boy I'd first met. He'd had his hair cut by a city barber, and his shoes were shined beyond regulation requirements. I feared for him. Coronation Street, the address he'd given, was the toughest part of Wabagoon. Run down hotels and boarding houses and cat houses and bootleggers abounded.

"Sam," I said, "I don't think I'd live there."

"Why not?" For the first time I noticed that Sam had a very firm jaw line.

"Well, you know, it's not exactly the best part of town."

"Mrs. Knox told me all about that. They were real well-off before the Depression. Had a big house over on Rosewood Crescent and servants even, and a cottage up at Enders Lake."

"And they lost it all in the crash."

"Yeah. How did you know? So they're living where they are until Mr. Knox gets this deal going out at the coast he's working on."

I didn't say any more. Maybe it was all true, and maybe there is a Santa Claus who brings goodies to good kids and maybe there is a fairy godmother with a beautiful daughter. Besides, it was none of my business. I joined the navy to get to sea, not to look after gullible farm boys.

We were joined by Mike and Mike was mad.

"How do you like that?" he snarled. "That sonovabitch Lightson. Boy. Know what he did?"

"I've a feeling we're going to find out."

"You know he asked me to report to him at Stand Easy."

"Yeah."

"I thought maybe he was going to give me shit about, you know, what I said, see. But first off he was as nice as pie. All smiles."

"Beware of a chief petty officer who is all smiles."

"You're not kidding. Anyway, he starts out talking to me real nice. Asks me where I'm from and how many brothers and sisters I got and all that, and then he asks me if I'd like to be captain of the heads."

"What is that?"

"Wait till I get to it." A natural story-teller, Mike liked to build suspense. "I thought, jees that's nice and I said sure. Know what the heads are?"

"Nope."

"Cans! Toilets! Don't you guys know nothing? There's five of 'em in this whole damned ship, counting the one for the officers. And yours truly's in charge of the whole stinking works. Which means cleaning 'em out after you dirty buggers have crapped in 'em. Captain of the heads!"

He snorted with disgust and spat on the floor – the deck – which was also strictly forbidden. I could see that Mike was in for trouble.

The bosun piped Fall In and we all lined up again in three ranks. Leading Seaman Yorny, a tall, powerful Swede, walked up and down in front of us. "Pull in the stomach. Straighten the line here. Move over half a step to the right, all of you. You're too close. That's it. Now the C.O. is going to talk to you so try to look like sailors and not a bunch of slobs."

So we did our best to look like sailors and not a bunch of slobs and out from the front – the upper deck – came the C.O. This was my first real look at Lieutenant Gridley. He was a young man, not more than twenty-five, the son of a Vancouver businessman, and he'd been in the reserve navy for four or five years before the war began. His doeskin uniform was so neat, his shirt so white, his starched collar so stiff, his cap so straight. And under his arm, so help me, he carried a telescope. I half expected him to suddenly put it to his eye and gaze out to sea, spot a sub and order the bosun to pipe Battle Stations.

Yorny saluted him smartly and the C.O. returned the salute. Then he turned to us.

"All right, men, stand easy."

We stood easy and waited.

Gridley's fresh, boyish face broke into a friendly smile. "Welcome to the navy. You have become part of the oldest and proudest military force in the British Empire. Part of the greatest navy in the world. Nelson's navy." I was beginning to feel a little tingle of pride. "And you know the signal that

Nelson made to his fleet at the Battle of Trafalgar. Every schoolboy knows it. 'England expects that every man will do his duty.' That's all. Do his duty. Always remember that you are part of that navy. I don't mean to downgrade the army or the air force, but you are navy. The senior service. There's a responsibility goes with that. It should show in the way you stand, the way you walk, the way you wear your uniform. You are navy."

There was a slight stiffening of every backbone as he said this.

"All right then," he went on. "You'll be here six weeks, during which time we will teach you many things. But what you really want, what I want, what we all want, is to get to sea. To get on a corvette or a minesweeper or a cruiser and get out there and chase the rotten, filthy German submarines off the sea. It's not easy, life at sea. It's cold and windy and rough and dangerous. Remember that when your training here seems rough and dangerous. But I want to tell you something. Already it has become evident that the boys from the prairies can take it when the going gets rough on the North Atlantic.

"But it is not all work and training here. We want you to have some fun. Work hard and play hard. We will have sports of all kinds. We hope to have a hockey team that will win the provincial championship. And softball and boxing and football. Have fun, but always remember, your real task is to kill Germans.

"Good luck and good hunting."

He turned and marched briskly back towards the front offices and we stood there, part of Nelson's Navy. And we were never allowed to forget it. The spirit of Horatio Nelson hovered over that old converted garage as surely as it did over HMS *Hood* or any other great ship in the British Navy.

At lunch time we met Smiley.

We were given a victualling allowance so that we could eat ashore. This meant going down Regal Avenue to a greasy spoon called the Empire Café, run by a long-suffering Chinaman called Charlie, where we could get a fairly decent lunch for thirty-five cents. It included potatoes, a pork chop or piece of beef or fried liver and onions or a piece of fish, green peas or boiled carrots, coffee and a piece of apple pie. Today for thirty-five cents you're lucky if you can get the coffee.

We had just gone ashore and were walking down the street in hot sunshine when a voice yelled from behind.

"Hey, you guys. Just a minute."

We turned and there coming towards us was a short, trim man in what we took to be an officer's uniform. We were just drawing ourselves up to salute when we noticed the lack of cap badge and sleeve stripes and stopped in time.

"Almost got you there," the newcomer grinned. He was a compact man who looked to be about thirty-five, with a lean face and rather long jaw. He walked with a certain weaving grace that I later found came from carrying trays in the dining rooms of CPR ships where he had worked for years as a waiter.

"My name's Bert Smiley," he said. "Mind if I join you?"

We didn't, of course, and told him our names as we shoved into a booth in the café. Sam was examining Smiley's sleeve badge. Two triangles with the letters OS inside.

"Officer's Steward," Smiley explained.

"You work in the wardroom?"

"I run the wardroom. Keep it clean, serve drinks, look after officers' laundry, wipe the Old Man's nose, if he so requires."

"Jees," Mike was impressed. "You must get to know quite a bit about them."

"I get to know all about them. Who their girl friends are, here and at home, wherever they come from."

"Gosh. What are they like?"

"Okay, for the most part. Sometimes you get an officious type who treats you like a servant, but not often. The guy who does that is usually some joker who never had a dime in his life - maybe a salesman or insurance agent or something - and now he thinks he's hot stuff because he's got a bit of braid on his sleeve."

I was beginning to like Smiley. "Tell me," I asked, "these guys with the one narrow stripe on their arms, what are they?"

"Probies. Probational sub-lieutenants, to give them their full title. They passed an officers selection board somewhere and then took a course at Cornwallis to learn to be officers."

"You mean they never been to sea or nothing?" Sam asked.

"Nope. Most of them are just out of school. From Toronto or Vancouver or wherever. Some from right here. They had a selection board six months ago and got about ten. Compared to Binns, for instance, they don't know a thing."

"Who's Binns?"

"Haven't you run into Petty Officer Binns yet? No, I guess you wouldn't but you will. He's that sort of pudgy guy who's about forty-five years old. Englishman. Joined the Royal Navy as a boy, went all through the last war. He really *is* navy."

"How come he never made officer?"

"Practically nobody from the ranks ever gets to be a commissioned officer. It's possible but rarely happens. No, you get to be an officer by being picked as an officer. Education has a lot to do with it. And officer-like qualities."

"Such as what?"

"Damned if I know. I've worked with hundreds of officers and as far as I can see they're just like anybody else. Some good, some bad. But that's par for the course in any outfit."

"Do you like them?" Mike asked.

"Some I like, some I detest."

"Which ones?"

Smiley just looked at him without saying a word.

"I suppose they all drink like fish?" Mike suggested.

"Listen, my friend, one thing an officers' steward doesn't do, if he wants to remain an officers' steward, is blab about his officers. Now speaking of drinking, how's about we go down to the Imperial tonight and have ourselves a few buckets of suds."

I agreed that this would be a good idea. Sam demurred and Mike had some other plans.

We were dismissed early that afternoon and, while most of the newcomers went about attending to things that needed attending to, Smiley and I headed for the beer parlour and my first public appearance in a naval uniform.

3

It's in the Fan

"Here's to war!" Smiley raised his tall glass on high. It was filled with beautiful amber Bohemian lager beer. Nectar of the gods. And on the small round table in front of each of us sat ten more glasses of the same.

We were seated in the gloomy dirty beer parlour of the Imperial Hotel. The place was full of round tables like ours, jammed so close together that the white-aproned waiters carrying round trays of beer aloft could scarcely weave their way between them. The tables were crowded with soldiers, airmen, and sailors, and a sprinkling of civilians (no women; they weren't yet permitted to drink in public), quaffing beer, swearing, shouting, arguing, laughing and generally enjoying themselves as they hadn't been able to do in the past ten years.

Smiley and I had, as they say, established rapport, which means that he'd told me about himself, which was interesting, and I'd told him about myself, which was dull.

Let me see, Smiley must have been over thirty years of age at the time. He'd come to Canada from England at the age of sixteen and had done just about everything. Worked in a lumber camp in B.C., in a mine in Sudbury, farmed briefly in Manitoba, got himself married and unmarried in the course of six months. Finally he'd landed a job as a steward on a CPR liner, where he'd made good money until the Depression hit and people stopped travelling on ocean liners. Then, like the rest of us, he'd become a bum.

"Now tell me about you," he said.

"Nothing much. School, hockey, baseball. Oh yeah, I had a paper route through high school."

"Ever been laid?"

"Sure, lots of times."

"Really?"

"No, not really. Too scared, I guess. Didn't want to get a dose or knock some girl up. Our Sunday School teachers could paint a pretty dismal picture of the wages of sin."

"Well, we'll have to remedy that, and soon." Then he lost interest in my sex life and, raising his glass aloft again, shouted, "Here's to war, mankind's favourite sport!"

I looked lovingly at the array of beer in front of me, and the more I drank the more clear-headed I became. I was filled with euphoria, wisdom, and a sense of peace.

"Yes, sir," Smiley went on with satisfaction. "In war everybody is happy. A licence to indulge ourselves in three of mankind's favourite pursuits: hunting, killing and chasing women. Not to mention pushing other people around.

"Business types dote on war. Demand is up and supply is down. And no more of this nonsense of people going on strike.

"Farmers are rubbing their hands with glee. From having nobody wanting their produce to people lining up for it. Giving ration coupons for it. Train loads of beef carcasses going to military camps to be chomped up by hungry fighters."

When Smiley got going there was no stopping him.

"Husbands love war because it gets them away from the dullness of wife and family. Wives love it because it gets the old man out of the house and out of town and opens the way for all sorts of titillating adventures.

"Girls love it. All these guys with money in their pockets just looking for a place to spend it. Preachers find new themes for sermons, politicians new uses for crud about sacrifice and patriotism and the great common cause. War gets voters off the politicians' backs about such petty concerns as fraud and graft and corruption.

"Young guys who have flat feet or colour blindness or are deaf in one ear or for some other reason can't join in the real fun find plenty of fun at home. Better jobs, fast promotion, lonely women, more money.

"The whole country suddenly knows where it's at. From all the petty nit-picking and jealousies and feuds, everybody starts pulling together for the common good. It's so good after all the psychological crap and bleeding heart thinking of the thirties to know where we stand. Four square on the side of God and the king and you can't beat that."

"And I say bullshit to that!"

We both looked, somewhat taken back, at the third man at our table whom we'd been completely ignoring. When we first sat down we'd greeted him in a friendly way, but he'd only grunted, brooding over his beer.

Now I took a good look at him and saw that he definitely had a lean and hungry look. I'd seen the type before. They knocked on back doors sullenly asking if the housewife would exchange a piece of bread for a mown lawn or some split wood. The look in their eyes was like that of a trapped wolf, hurt, defiant, humiliated and filled with hate. To quote Robert Service, my favourite poet of the twenties, "a face most hair and the dreary stare of a dog whose day is done." Where they came from nobody knew; where they went nobody cared.

But with Smiley's flamboyant description of war, a spark of rebellion had returned to his tired eyes.

"Bullshit!" he repeated.

"Well, well, another country heard from." Smiley beamed on the stranger fondly, his glass still raised. "For a while there I thought you were either dead or asleep. What have you got against war?"

"Just that it's arranged by the capitalist bastards who run this country, and the rest of the world for that matter."

"Maybe so, maybe so." Smiley took another pull of his beer. "But isn't everything else? Tell you what war does for the country, it gets money moving around again. Money's no good unless it's moving from pocket to pocket, and providing some fun along the way."

"Bullshit!" was our tablemate's only comment.

"If you joined one of the services, they'd fix those teeth for you, free," Smiley, always the pragmatist, suggested.

"What good are teeth if you get your head blown off?" Before Smiley could comment on the wisdom of that statement, our ragged companion continued, getting more worked up the more he talked. "Fight for king and country! That's a laugh. What the hell did the king or the country either ever do for me?"

"Aha, touché! I'll admit you have a point there, my friend, but you are looking at it the wrong way. Just consider what your country is willing – nay anxious – to do for you now. Besides fixing those teeth, there's travel and excitement and girls and fun. All the adventures that are frowned on in civilian life are applauded by the military, up to and including adultery."

"That's the way they suck you in!" Our friend was becoming very red in the face. He pounded the table, causing a considerable amount of consternation among the assembled glasses of beer. From the corner of my eye I saw the effect of this on four fledgling airmen sitting at the next table. They didn't like it.

"Fight for king and country? Ha!" our lean friend scoffed. "Where were they when we were looking for jobs and getting our asses kicked off freight trains? To hell with the king, and the country, too!"

This was too much for a young airman with an earnest face and a crew cut who was sitting back to back with our friend.

"Cut out that kind of talk, you damned zombie," he threatened, "or I'll cut it out for you!"

"Now now," Smiley admonished. "Let us remember that free speech is one of the principles for which we are fighting." And then, obviously pleased with this bit of rhetoric, he continued, "Although I disagree with this man, I'll fight to the death to defend his right to say it."

"You damned betcha!" I shouted. The nectar of the gods was beginning to have an opposite effect. From a benign pussycat, I was becoming a tiger with blood in its eye.

"Oh yeah?" another airman, bigger than the first and more full of beer, shouted and jumped to his feet.

Realizing in my fuzzy brain that if I was to continue this brilliant repartee on anything like equal terms I couldn't do it sitting down, I too leaped to my feet.

My timing was awful for at that precise moment a waiter with a full tray, which he was holding out at almost arm's length, happened to have it straight above my head. When my head hit the bottom of the tray, as the proverbial stuff hits the proverbial fan, all that gorgeous golden brew went spraying over the heads of six airmen.

Always a reasonable man, I began to explain to the gentlemen just how the accident had happened, but Smiley had hold of me by the arm and was hissing, "Come on. Scram!"

I grabbed our lean, ragged friend by the arm in a similar fashion and, without further cavil, we got the hell out of there. From the street we could hear that a certain amount of pandemonium had developed behind us and we dispersed in all directions. A late streetcar came clanking to a stop at the corner and I jumped aboard. Thus ended, ignominiously, my first combat in uniform.

The next morning I slept in and woke with a foul taste in my mouth and a head that felt as though a truck had run over it.

I got into my uniform and ran all the way to the ship, but when I came aboard they were already singing "Eternal Father Strong to Save" and I had to wait through the Lord's Prayer and the other prayers from the Anglican Prayer Book and then I was in the shit.

I'd been briefed on naval discipline in one of the early lectures. It was all spelled out in the navy bible known as K.R. and A.I., which means King's Regulations and Admiralty Instructions. In this thick book were all the rules by which we must live, and the punishments that we must suffer if we broke any of the rules.

These punishments ranged all the way from Number Eleven to Dishonourable Discharge. Number Eleven was the standard punishment in a reserve division, which HMCS *Porpoise* was. It meant confinement to the ship with extra duty for one or more days. A mild punishment, but the navy wasn't out to break anybody's spirit and there were no Captain Blys in the Canadian service.

So I was paraded to the quarterdeck, a small space by the side door where the ship's bell was and where a small altar was set up, behind which Commanding Officer Gridley stood.

"Step forward and state your name and number," the C.P.O. barked, and I stepped forward and did so.

The C.O. looked at me, trying to appear stern but it was almost beyond his capacity. Western Canadians, in fact Canadians generally, have never been accustomed to heel-clicking discipline.

"Well, Diespecker," he said, "it didn't take you long to get into trouble. What happened?"

My head hurt terribly. "I was drunk last night, sir."

"I see. Well, drunkenness is no crime in itself, you understand, but being late for morning roll call is. Punctuality is important in the navy."

"Yes, sir."

He could see how much my head hurt, I'm sure. "Two days Number Eleven," he stated loudly in his best imitation of a stern naval commander. "Dismissed."

So I saluted and took the two steps back, turned as briskly as I could and marched away.

"Report to my office," Lightson hissed as I passed him.

So while the other recruits were marching, being lectured, learning to present arms, I went to Lightson's office at the very stern of the ship, behind the canteen. I stood outside the door and waited.

Finally he came. He went into the office and sat down behind a battered desk while I stood at attention in front of it. "Do you know what happens tomorrow morning, Saturday, at o-nine hundred, Diespecker?"

"No, sir."

"Don't call me sir. I told you that. Can't you get anything through your thick skull?"

It came as a bit of a shock to be chewed out. We just weren't used to it. Even in school, the only other dictatorship I knew of, teachers were a bit more subtle in their scoldings. Not being able to say sir I didn't know what to say.

Lightson went on. "Well, tomorrow at o-nine hundred is a little ceremony known as Captain's Rounds. At which time the Captain, followed by the chief engineer, which we don't have, and the M.O., which we do have, and the executive officer and the officer of the day and myself and last of all Petty Officer Binns go over this ship inch by inch to make sure that everything is ship shape. Understand?"

"Yes, uh, yes."

"You can call me Chief. Everybody else does."

"Yes, Chief."

A friendly smile flicked across his handsome face and then he went on. "And believe you me, Deeeees-pecker, they inspect this ship. The Captain wears white gloves and he runs his finger along every door jamb and behind every capstan, everywhere, from stem to stern. And if he finds one speck of dust it's my ass, and that means your ass. Understand?"

"Yes."

"So your job is to clean this ship. The work party will help you during duty hours, but after that you are on your own. That means polishing all the brass, scrubbing the decks that are fit to be scrubbed, waxing the wardroom deck. You do that late at night when nobody's using the wardroom. Understand?"

"Yes." Gawd, how my head ached.

"And you'll do it perfectly. Nothing short of perfection is good enough in this navy. You'll take your meals here and you'll sleep here. Binns will instruct you in slinging your hammock."

"For how long?"

"Two days. That's Friday night and Saturday night."

"Yes, sir." It was out before I could stop it.

Lightson's thin lips pressed together. "Dees-pecker, are you trying to be smart with me?"

"No, no, of course not. It just sort of . . ."

"Because, if you are," he continued, "let me warn you it won't wash."

I was trying desperately not to look at his face, but I couldn't seem to keep my eyes off it. So I stared past him at a picture of a battleship on the wall.

"Pay attention!" Lightson snapped. "And let me tell you something. There is absolutely no place for a smart alec in this man's navy."

Oh Lord. This man's navy. I had the feeling I was in a bad First World War movie, but this was real.

Lightson was still glaring at me. "Dismissed, Deespecker," he roared. "Smartly now!"

I almost brought up a salute, but stopped myself in time. I made as good an about turn as I could manage and got out of there.

My two buddies cornered me at Stand Easy where I was standing in the recreation room chewing on a Sweet Marie bar and drinking a coke. So help me, I've never eaten so much candy or drunk so many soft drinks as I did aboard *Porpoise*. Always at Stand Easy it was a chocolate bar and a coke. I suppose we needed the energy for all the marching, rope-climbing, boat-pulling and running we did in between times.

"What happened?" Mike wanted to know.

"Yeah." Real concern creased Sam's broad face. "How did it go?"

Several other ratings had joined us and I saw I had an audience, and to have an audience was to perform. I drew myself up into a rigid imitation of C.P.O. Lightson and tried out my best limey accent.

"Naow see 'ere, Dyes-picker. I haint tyking no sarse from the lykes of yew. Ainey lolligagging or skylarkin on yer part and oil personally see to hit that yer flogged with the cat-o-nine-tyles, keel-hauled and 'anged from the yawd harm."

Not good, but I had a select audience and they roared their approval. Applause was like catnip to a cat and I continued my act. Taking a peaked cap from the hand of a writer standing nearby, I stuck it on my head, thrust out my chin and went on.

"Yassur, me lad, yer goin to learn who runs this 'ere ship. Not those snot-nosed officers who wouldn't know a battleship from a bathtub, but me. Hunderstand?" I threw out my chest, pulled in my stomach and clicked my heels. "Lightning Lightson, that 'oo"

But this time there was no laughter. Only dead silence. Mike and Sam were looking extremely pained and Mike was motioning ever so slightly with his thumb to a point directly behind me. Without looking I knew my audience had been increased by one. It couldn't be Lightson. It just couldn't be. He'd been in the canteen. I saw him there.

"Very funny indeed, Dees-pecker," a cool voice said quietly, and then, somewhat louder, "Turn around when I'm talking to you!"

I turned around. Lightson's face was white and drawn, lips tight, his eyes hard. I thought he was going to hit me, but a seasoned navy man like him would never hit a rating. Instead, not trusting himself to say more, he turned and marched off. My audience sort of slunk away, no doubt feeling a terrible sense of guilt by association.

As for me, if I'd felt sick before, I felt ten times as sick now. The nickname "Lightning" would, I knew, stick with him.

So, in the space of a few days I had antagonized the one man in the navy whom no one should ever, under any circumstances, antagonize.

38

4

Captain's Rounds

There are some decks that, no matter how hard you sweep them, never come clean. Such was the concrete deck of HMCS *Porpoise*. The entire ship's company went to work on it with brooms and mops first thing Friday morning after opening services.

First we swept it, then we washed it down with hoses, over and over again and then mopped it, but that old garage floor still came up dusty. The same with the wooden deck in the recreation room. The accumulated dust and grime of years lay beneath that hardwood flooring, and the more you swept off the surface the more came up between the cracks.

But it, too, was scrubbed and waxed and made to look as presentable as possible. And every bit of brass on the ship was polished until it reflected the pained face of the rating doing the work. The big brass bell on the quarterdeck on which the quartermaster solemnly donged out the one bell, two bells, on up to eight bells. The brass on the twelve-pounder cannon that stood beside the quarterdeck, to remind us that this was indeed a ship of war and not a garage; the brass of the big round compass; the brass on the capstan; even the brass on the big boiler where we boiled coffee for the canteen. Everything that could be shined was shined.

Paint was applied liberally to the front of the canteen, the rotting window sills, or rather porthole rims, the door jambs, everything that could take paint. Doggedly the entire ship's company, looking like a group of workmen in their fatigues, laboured all day.

About halfway through the morning I reported to Petty Officer Binns to learn how to sling my hammock. He was a short, wiry, leather-faced man with a walk that showed he spent more time on ships than on land. He was quiet and polite and considerate and never raised his voice. Harry Binns represented everything that was good about the navy.

"All right, lad, there is really nothing to slinging a hammock." He took hold of mine and rolled it out on the deck. "This," he said, pointing, "is called the head of the mick, this other end the foot. These thin lines attached to the ends are called nettles and they pass through this metal ring here, through which the lanyard is spliced. Okay. Important thing in slinging a hammock is to make sure to give the centre nettles about one and a half inches more scope than the side ones. Otherwise you'll get pitched out on the deck."

Deftly he placed the bite of the lanyard over the hammock hood and triced up the foot to the right height, securing it with a double sheet bend. His fingers flew through the knots. When he saw my amazed admiration, he said, "Nothing to it, lad, you'll be doing it better than I before you leave here."

After all the others had left – gone ashore – I sat down on a bench in the recreation room to eat some dry sandwiches. Smiley poked his head around the door.

"There you are," he chirped. "How's the head?"

"Terrible. How's yours?"

"Not bad. I was able to have a hair of the dog before anybody showed up this morning. Hear you had a run-in with Lightning Lightson."

"Yeah. Two days Number Eleven."

"Come with me. Nobody in the wardroom right now. I'll fix you a little something in my galley."

Smiley's galley was a four-by-six space partitioned off with plywood just outside the back door of the wardroom. In it he had a frig, a stove, a sink, and a counter.

"You'd be surprised what I can whip up in this little place," he said. "Want some coffee?"

"That would be great."

He poured black coffee and kept an alert ear for anyone entering the wardroom while I drank it.

"One piece of advice," Smiley said, watching me. "Don't make fun of Lightson's accent. Everybody wants to but nobody does it. He'll get you."

"Well, it's only six weeks."

"Six weeks! Who are you kidding? Lightson has the say on who gets drafted out of here. He can keep you in this hole for the duration!"

"Like hell he can! There must be some justice, even in the navy."

Smiley leaned against the sink in his galley and gave me a knowing look. "How old are you anyway, Dink?"

"Twenty."

"Twenty, eh? And you've lived through the Depression and you've been unemployed. Seen men who had built up good jobs and homes suddenly left with nothing. Seen guys clubbed by railway cops for no other reason except they were unemployed. And you still talk about justice?"

"Well, you know."

"Sure, I know, you're young and you've been through the Sunday School, Boy Scouts, Mother's Day, and apple pie, and you find it hard to give up all these glorious ideas of justice and fair play and all men being equal before the law. Let me tell you."

I had to stop him. I remembered that when Smiley got going he was good for hours. "Anyway, I'm damned well not going to hang around this dump scrubbing floors and scrubbing out heads just because I made one little mistake."

"Well, lots of luck, lots of luck."

Somebody came into the wardroom and yelled for Smiley. I got the hell out of there, picked up my bucket and scrub brush, and headed for the offices to begin the night's work.

Two hours later, when I'd finished the C.O.'s office and the recruiting office and was just beginning on the general office, the door from the lower deck opened and a young man came in. He wasn't any older than I was but he sure looked different. Everything about him shone, half-Wellington boots, doeskin uniform, and the rest. Only his cap showed he was human. In common with the other young officers, he'd taken the hard ring out of it so that it slouched to one side, just enough, you understand, to give him that salty look. He was taller than I and solidly built. I can only describe him as bursting with health and muscles. His face was rather heavy, with a straight nose and a wide mouth with a set to it that I couldn't quite figure at the moment.

He parked his backside on the desk, dangled a boot near my nose and said, "That looks like hard work."

I stopped scrubbing and looked up at him from my kneeling position. Then, remembering I was in the navy, jumped to my feet and brought up a perfect salute. This nonplussed him some because he had to stand up then and return the salute.

"Okay, okay, at ease - or whatever. Sit down. Let's shoot the breeze a bit."

"Okay." I sat down. "But I've got to get all this done for Captain's Rounds or Lightson will -" I stopped.

He didn't seem to appreciate my position, but sat on the corner of the desk again.

"I'm the officer of the day. My name's Egheart, Tom Egheart. What's yours?"

"Diespecker." Egheart? Egheart? I knew that name. Yeah, it was plastered all over the furniture stores in town, the best furniture stores, very expensive furniture that was as much a part of Canada as Heintzman pianos.

"You wouldn't be -"

"Yeah." He said it simply with no bravado. Just yes, I'm the millionaire you know, a bore really. I'd never met a millionaire before, or a thousandaire for that matter. I looked him over. Here was a guy from another world, a world I knew nothing about. Toronto, manufacturing, money, private school, probably. About my age, a Canadian like me, but there the similarity ended.

"Where you from, Diespecker?"

"Right here. Lived here all my life. Born here. Went to school here." I was being defensive and I didn't want to be.

"You mean you've never been away from here?"

"Not far. Out Doron way, threshing. To Vancouver and back, riding the rods. Never been east of Winnipeg in my life."

"Jesus!" He looked appalled, then realizing how it must have appeared to me, softened it. "Well, now that you're in the navy you will."

"That's why I joined."

He grinned a very boyish grin, very sincere, and something else. "You mean fighting for king and country had nothing to do with it, or making the world safe for democracy?"

"As the fellow says, 'Fugg that.' "

He laughed. "Well, that's interesting."

I was hot and I was tired and I was hung over and I was thoroughly pissed off with a lot of things, and so my tongue got away from me. "Look, that king and country crap may mean a lot to you. This country's done all right by you, but it's done bugger all for me."

His smile had gone, replaced by a quizzical, interested look. "But surely, Hitler and the German treatment of the Jews and the violation of international law – "

He was right, of course, at least partly right. But I've always enjoyed an argument and I hadn't had a good one in a long time. And the first principle of arguing is not to admit that anything your adversary says has a tiny grain of truth in it.

"What does that mean? Hell, the British have been doing it for centuries, taking over India, large chunks of Africa, North America – the Indians never invited them here – whenever it suited their purpose. And when people rebelled they killed them. You must have heard of the Indian Mutiny. Or, for that matter, Mackenzie's Rebellion."

He looked surprised. "You're an intelligent man, Diespecker."

"Oh yes, there are a few intelligent people west of Ontario."

"Hey, cut it out, will you."

43

"Okay, okay, I'm overdoing it. You're right. But, Jesus, I feel terrible."

"Yeah, I can understand it. Hey, how about a cup of coffee? Sorry I can't invite you into the wardroom, but we can drink it in here."

"A beer would go a lot better."

"Yeah." He'd taken his cap off and now he ran his hand through his sandy hair. "Why not? As officer of the day I've got keys to everything, even Smiley's stores. Sit tight and I'll bring us a beer each."

He got up and walked smartly through the wardroom door, and I thought, He's taking a chance. I could report this or we could get caught.

The beer helped a lot. Tom told me some things about himself and we got on the subject of sports.

"What do you play?" he wanted to know.

"Everything. Hockey. I played goal for the collegiate team and tried out for the Wabagoon Juniors. Baseball. I'm a catcher."

"Skiing?"

"Nope. Not many hills around here. Do you ski?"

"Oh yes. Down hill, slalom, cross country." I'd never heard of any of these. "How about swimming?" he asked.

"Some. But there's not much water, either."

"Hmm. How about boxing? The Old Man's hot on sports and he's made me sports officer. He's going to want to - to use his term - beat the ass off the air force and the army in every sport. Right now he's hot on boxing."

"I boxed some in the athletic club at high school."

"Good. You're about a middleweight, I'd say. We boxed at Upper Canada and it was a big thing at the naval college where we took our basic training." He was looking at me, sizing me up. "I enjoy boxing. How about a little go?"

"What? You mean now? Me and you?"

"Sure. I'll get the gloves out of the sports locker and we can fool around a bit."

Anything was better than scrubbing. "Okay, if you say so."

So we went out to the main deck and he got the gloves out. He removed his uniform jacket and took off his collar and tie and white shirt, and I could see that he looked pretty strong. I didn't remove anything because all I had on was the work fatigues and my underwear shorts. We must have made a strange-looking pair.

He had a classic, stand-up style with his left extended and his right held in front of his chest. I'd been taught by a semi-pro boxer to fight in a crouch with both hands in front of me so as to be ready to hit with either one. Well, we circled around a bit self-consciously and the next thing I knew his left shot out and caught me on the cheek bone. It hurt and I knew I'd better watch that left. But no matter how much I watched it it kept flicking out fast and catching me, usually high on the head. He never followed with his right, perhaps not wanting to hurt me.

So I started circling to get away from the left. If he'd just get that right arm away from his midsection I might do something. Then he did it. Threw a left jab, which I took on my left glove, and then swung a looping right. I stepped inside it and hit him with all I had in the solar plexis. Maybe all my resentment was in that punch. Anyway, it was much harder than I'd intended and it caught him right on the button. His arms dropped to his sides, his face went white and he doubled up and sat on his ass gasping for breath.

I shook my gloves off and started to help him up.

"Gosh, I'm sorry."

He shook his head, still unable to speak, and so I left him there. After a few more seconds he climbed shakily to his feet, still white, still gasping.

"You sure suckered me into that. Whew! Man, oh man." He was shaking the gloves off his hands.

I figured I was in more trouble than ever. I didn't know much about the navy but I was pretty sure striking an officer was against some rule or other. Maybe I'd be court martialed.

But Sub-Lieutenant Egheart was only grinning sheepishly. "Next time I'll try to be ready for that one. Your style, it confused me." He put on his shirt and jacket. "I know one thing anyway. I've got a middleweight for my boxing team."

"Me?"

"None other."

So now I was going to get my head pounded by somebody I didn't even hate. Right now I had a bigger problem. How to get those floors waxed before morning. I knew Sub-Lieutenant Egheart wasn't about to help me.

At seven o'clock when Lightson came breezing into the office I was just finishing waxing the last floor.

"What in hell took you so long?" he wanted to know.

"I'm not feeling my usual speedy best."

"I guess not. Well, get your ass out of here and join the work party. There's a hell of a lot to be done before Captain's Rounds at o-nine hundred."

I joined the work party.

Captain's Rounds. When I think of them now they become confused with a Christopher Robin parade with the little boy and the teddy bear and the donkey and the kangaroo all marching along so straight, heads up, arms swinging, filled with pomp and ceremony. The C.O. came first, strutting along like the Prince of Wales inspecting a troop of Hottentots, and then the first lieutenant or Number One, as he was called, then the medical officer, trying not to look foolish, and then the paymaster – I never could figure out why Pay is in on it – followed by Chief Petty Officer Lightson, carrying a clip board to note all the things that weren't shipshape, then Binns, the head of the work party, the low man on the totem pole onto whose shoulders all the crap filtered down the line from the Captain.

I watched them parade through the fore body of the ship, the Captain peering into cupboards and seamens' lockers and the canteen and the recreation room, running his white-gloved finger along ledges, then looking at it and frowning and shaking his head. How, I wondered, could grown men take this ridiculous charade seriously? But then in wartime all reason seems to be suspended and ridiculous things are done – like killing people.

They finished up in the main part of the ship, with Lightson taking copious notes, all of which he'd later toss in the wastebasket with a grunt of disgust. Then they marched towards the office and suddenly I had a horrible feeling. That damned beer bottle. In a defiant moment I'd tossed it into a wastepaper basket. Christ, if the C.O. found that, Lightson would never let up on me.

What to do? Couldn't pass them in the narrow passageway. But if the C.O. stopped to check something along the way I might make it by nipping out the side door and in the front. So, without asking permission to go ashore, I made the dash, out the door, down the street, around the corner and in the front door. A writer was alone in the office and he looked up in some surprise. Ratings were never, repeat *never*, to use that front door.

"What the hell?" he began, springing to his feet. I brushed past him, grabbed the wastebasket off the floor, set it on the desk and began rummaging through it, just as Christopher Robin and his train came through the door. The Captain stopped and they all stopped behind him, jammed into the narrow passageway. He didn't say anything, just looked at me.

I mumbled, "Lost something," set the basket down on the floor and retreated hell bent out through the front door again. As I went I heard the Captain say, "Have that man report to me!" I was in the shit again.

5

The Wardroom Party

So it was two more days Number Eleven. My weekend was already ruined. While my shipmates were free to have fun like finding new girlfriends or going swimming or whatever, I had to hang around that hot, dirty, scruffy barracks. Perhaps the hardest part was explaining to my mother why I wouldn't be home. Her first remark when I phoned her was, "Robin, have you been doing something wrong?"

"No, not really, Ma. It's just, well you know, the navy."

"Well, I don't know." Her voice was full of worry. For as long as she lived, no matter where they were or what they were doing, Mother lived in constant fear that one of her kids would do Something Wrong.

"Do you want me to get your father to speak to the commanding officer?" she asked.

"No, for Ch - for goodness sake, don't do that! Look, Ma, I've got to go now."

"Well, all right. Good-bye."

My next project, since Lightson had gone ashore and there was no immediate duty for me to perform, was to get some sleep. I tried the hammock but after falling out of it three times I curled up on the battered old chesterfield and fell into the first sleep I'd had in two days.

I had hardly closed my eyes when somebody started shaking me. I stared up at the hatchet face of Smiley.

"Come on, Dink," he said. "I need you."

"What time is it?"

"Almost eight."

"Can't be. I just closed my eyes."

"Listen, I looked in on you four times and you were pounding your ear so hard I thought it was a foghorn."

I sat up and rubbed my eyes. "Hungry," I yawned.

"Okay, I'll give you something to eat. But you've got to hurry. Get into the head and shave and then into your dress blues and report to me."

"Smiley, for crying out loud! You sound like an officer."

"Never mind that crap, Dink. I need you. They're having a big party in the wardroom. You help me and we'll have our own party afterwards. There's always enough unfinished drinks to make ten ratings drunk."

"That sounds better. What do I have to do?"

"Stay in the galley and mix drinks, and if things get too hectic later on, maybe carry a trayful or two in. I tell you it can be a lot of fun."

"How?"

"Well, some of these officers' wives and girlfriends get pretty high and pretty friendly. After about midnight everybody forgets what kind of a uniform you've got on. Last party Ordinary Seaman Wilson – he's gone now – was dancing on the table in the recreation room with Nancy McGill. She's the recruiting officer's wife and a real lively one, and then they disappeared and nobody asked any questions."

"How about the recruiting officer?"

"He was too busy chasing the executive officer's girl-friend. Then around about two in the morning, the Captain does his thing."

"What's that?"

He gave me that sharp look of his. "You'll just have to wait and find out."

Well, Smiley had made it all sound so interesting that by now I was eager to be his assistant. Besides, I wasn't going anywhere.

So I did as Smiley advised. Shaved, showered, got out my

dress blues from my locker and with an iron borrowed from Smiley even pressed the collar and dicky and took the creases out of the trousers. Gave my boots the greatest shine they'd ever had, cleaned the grime of HMCS *Porpoise* from my finger-nails and applied a little Brylcreem to my unruly locks. The result, except for some bags under my eyes, wasn't too bad.

Smiley was busier'n a cat on a tin roof getting ready, fuss-ing about dusting the mantel, straightening drapes, fluffing cushions. And I helped him. The wardroom was a surprise to me. The furniture was old but good, the walls were panelled in oak, and above an imitation fireplace hung a picture of King George. Pictures of famous British battlewagons adorned the walls. Crossed swords were attached to the panelling. I began to get a feeling of the dignity and tradition of the navy.

Then we heard the front door open and Smiley hissed, "Out!" and I nipped out the door into the galley. With the door to the wardroom open, I could peek through the crack and see part of the room.

The officer who'd come in was one of the younger subbies, about my age, whom I recognized immediately as a Wabagoon boy who had been a big wheel at Patuna Collegiate. He'd gone to university while I'd joined the ranks of the unemployed. I remembered him as a cocky, egotistical, conceited civilian and now that he'd joined the navy I suspected he'd become a cocky, egotistical, unbearable officer.

But it was the girl with him that really got me. She stood inside the wardroom door across from where I was peeking just long enough for me to get a glimpse of a beautiful smile and a gorgeous figure. It was something like peeking through the viewer at a girly show in a fun house. Then she moved further into the wardroom and was gone from my field of vision. But I'd seen enough to upset me. She was my dream girl. Norma Shearer and Connie Bennett and Jean Harlow all rolled into one.

Smiley came bustling into the galley. "A double scotch for Hotshot. And straight ginger ale for Miss Reilly. Isn't she something though? Hotshot tried to signal me to slip a little gin into her drink, but to hell with him. He's been trying to make that mouse ever since he came here, but he's never had any luck. I don't think he ever will."

So I mixed the drinks and, for some dastardly reason, slipped a little extra scotch into Hotshot's drink. What he got was not a double, but more like a triple.

One by one the other officers arrived. Paymaster Boyd was one of the first. He was a short, smiling man who had been an accountant with one of the large farm implement companies and he really loved the navy. Everybody called him Pay, and he was popular with officers and ratings alike. The Captain came next with his wife, who was trim and svelte and stylish and gave off an air of country clubs and money. She was the daughter of one of the largest brewers in the west.

"Go a little easy with Susie's drink," Smiley instructed. He had names for all the wives and girlfriends, too, and treated the entire party as any good maitre d' should, with regard for all their little weaknesses and foibles. So I put in a little bit of gin and lots of ginger. The Captain was drinking rum and coke, which he called a Cubalibre.

"Make Doc a good stiff rye and water with ice." The Doc was Smiley's favourite among the officers, as he was with all the ratings. "And for Dora just about as stiff, but with ginger. That girl can really hold her booze. Good tough prairie stock there."

"What about Egheart?" I asked. Ever since our boxing episode I'd talked to him off and on and was beginning to like him.

"You mean Sub-Lieutenant Egheart," Smiley corrected. "Call the officers Joe Shit if you want when we're in the beer parlour with other ratings, but around here you give them their proper titles."

"Okay, okay."

"Besides, he's been elevated to First Lieutenant or Number One or Jimmy the One, whatever you want to call it, which means that he's next in authority to the Captain."

"So what does he drink?"

"Scotch, of course. With soda. No ice."

"And his lady?"

"Don't know. He brings a different one every time."

Then somebody shouted from the wardroom and Smiley was gone. I could hear him bustling about and soon he had me pouring drinks with both hands while he delivered them. Had to admire Smiley the way he could manoeuvre a tray of drinks out the door and through that crowd without spilling a drop. The pace speeded up and we didn't have much time for more conversation. I got to pondering the question of what makes an officer an officer and a rating a rating. It was sure new to me. I'd always considered myself as good as anybody alive, there being no class distinction on the prairies at that time, but now I was learning differently. It wasn't going to be easy.

Smiley came back into the galley, took a bottle of Chivas Regal from the cupboard where he kept it for his own use, poured a shot glass full and downed it. Then he popped a mint into his mouth to kill his breath.

"A rule," he said. "One drink every hour, not a drop more, helps you through the long night." He poured an ounce into the shot glass and handed it to me. I knocked it back and it damned near knocked me back. But I felt better.

The sounds of revelry from the wardroom increased in exact proportion to the drinks that were pouring in through the door. There was laughter and talk and stories and giggles and gossip and it was all pretty exciting to a new entry like me.

The size and number of the drinks increased. Hotshot in particular was knocking back the doubles at a great rate. Smiley was running faster and faster with trays. He got behind and said, "You take this one in."

"What will I do?"

"Just pass them around. They're too potted to know who's doing it."

So in I went with a tray full of glasses. The wardroom scene was interesting. Pay and the C.O. were throwing darts at a board on the wall. One of the junior officers had his jacket off and was demonstrating how many pushups he could do. The C.O.'s wife was rather red in the face, had her shoes off and was demonstrating to somebody how high she could kick. The others were sitting and talking animatedly, but it was Hotshot and Patricia Reilly who particularly caught my attention. He had her squeezed over as far as she could get on the big old chesterfield. He kept putting a big paw on her knee, and she kept removing it. I couldn't take my eyes off her. Now that I could get an unimpeded view she was a thousand times better than she'd appeared before. I can't describe her any better than saying that she glowed. A glow that filled the wardroom. I was surprised that people could sit around and not be staring at her.

When I got to where they were sitting, I held the glasses towards them. As Patricia went to take hers, Hotshot reached for it, snatched it from the tray and tasted it.

"There's no gin in that at all," he yelled. "Straight ginger ale."

"That's fine," she said. "Just the way I like it."

"What the hell is going on here, anyway?" He glared up at me. "And who in hell are you? You're not Smiley."

"Please, Walter," she protested.

He jumped to his feet and weaved unsteadily. "You're not even a steward!"

All the others had stopped talking or dart-throwing or pushups or kicking and were looking at us.

"Well?" he demanded.

"I'm helping Smiley out, sir."

"Oh you are, are you?" He opened his mouth full bore and roared, "Smiley!"

Smiley came bustling in from the galley. "Yes, sir."

"What the hell is this guy doing serving drinks?"

I had to admire Smiley. Calm, polite, reasonable.

"Is there anything wrong, sir?" he asked, without deference or scorn or rancour, but with dignity.

"This rating – whoever he is – why is he serving drinks?"

"He very kindly offered to help me. You see," he explained with great patience, "we don't have an assistant steward on strength, and when we have a, uh, special occasion, it's more than one man can handle."

But Hotshot was on his feet and he couldn't just let the matter drop. "Well, it's not right, not navy . . . not . . ."

The C.O. came over then. He was somewhat red in the face but as any good naval officer should be he was in complete control.

"It's all right, Sub-Lieutenant," he said, leaning just a bit on the *Sub*, "Smiley has my permission to get help. I think they both are doing an excellent job under the circumstances. That's all, Diespecker." As I turned to leave I heard him add, *soto voce*, "Sit down, you bloody fool."

Hotshot sat down.

Back in the galley, Smiley whispered, "He's a prick and there's nothing you can do about pricks when they have stripes on their arms."

I stayed in the galley for a while. But after Smiley's efforts, the party really started to get a glow on. They moved out of the wardroom into the recreation hall. Somebody put a dime in the juke box and the sweet strains of "The Music Goes Round and Round" soon filled the air. Everybody began to dance and Smiley and I were busy running back and forth from the galley to the recreation room with trays of glasses.

On one trip the juke box was rolling out "Hutsut Rolson on a Rillera and a Brawlabrawla Suit" and the dancing was getting wilder and wilder. Nancy was yelling, "I want to dance on the table. Who'll dance on the table with me?" She was referring to the long, sturdy table covered with battleship linoleum that occupied the centre of the recreation room. Everybody else was dancing and paying her no attention and it was just my luck to be handing her a drink.

"Come on, you cute little sailor boy," she cooed, "dance on the table with me."

By this time I'd had several smashes of Smiley's special, to calm my nerves, you understand, and I was in a bit of a reckless mood myself. So up on the table we climbed and danced, or at least staggered about, and it was with the greatest of difficulty that I kept the two of us from tumbling off onto the floor. Manoeuvring thus, I still tried to keep my eye on her husband. But I needn't have bothered. He completely ignored his wife tonight and busied himself with a cute little brunette who was

54

the escort of one of the probies who had passed out on the old chesterfield.

Dancing on a table presented several problems to me. I was never the most graceful person around and a couple more belts of Smiley's special hadn't helped my equilibrium. Besides there was Nancy. She was lean and willowy and she writhed. I'd danced close to girls before, of course, as close as nature would allow, but this was ridiculous. I was much aware of every bit of her delectable body from her firm breasts to her firm thighs and everything in between. This soon raised the biggest problem of all and the more Nancy became aware of it the more she writhed. Trying to fit my body around Nancy, maintain my footing on the slippery table top, retain some semblance of keeping in step and in time to the music proved altogether too much. After one particularly long and exultant swoop down the table, I lost my balance and started for the floor, still clutching Nancy. But we never hit it. Doc happened to be passing at the time with some young thing in his arms and he calmly let go of her and grabbed us.

Nancy screamed with laughter as though it had all been planned.

I was considerably shook up.

"If I were you, son," Doc said kindly, "I'd get back to the galley. This is a little rich for your blood."

I got back to the galley.

And then I did a foolish thing. I guess I should say another foolish thing. Our supply of glasses was getting low and I went into the wardroom to retrieve some empty ones, arriving just in time to interrupt Hotshot in the act of practically raping Miss Reilly, at least it looked that way to me. They sprang apart at my entrance and Hotshot, very red in the face, leaped to his feet.

"Diespecker, you stupid aws." In the navy barely six weeks and he'd already picked up an English accent. "What the hell do you come barging in here for?"

Now here was a dilemma. A very serious dilemma such as was encountered sooner or later by most men in the service. If this guy had called me "a stupid aws" under any other circumstance, I'd have belted him. Especially as I knew I could take him. He'd belonged to the collegiate athletic club for a while and I once boxed with him. He was nothing. Taking this kind of guff from a stranger was bad enough, but from somebody you knew in civilian life . . . well.

"I'm picking up the fuggin' glasses, if you want to know, sir."

Well now, add to barging in, swearing in the presence of an officer and an officer's lady.

Hotshot went very white. "I'll have your ass for this, Diespecker. You'll be sorry you ever – "

There we were, standing toe to toe, both drunk, me a little and he a lot. A terrible thing could have happened. Then darling Miss Reilly laid her hand gently on Hotshot's arm and in a sweet voice said, "I really would like a drink."

And at the exact same moment Smiley yelled from the galley.

"Dink! More glasses, on the double!"

"What the hell are you bucking for?" he demanded when I reached the galley. "To get on everybody's shit list in the first month?"

Every party reaches a climax and the climax of this one was when the C.O. did his thing. This consisted of having the quartermaster on duty prepare a blank charge for the twelve pounder, which would then be ceremoniously hauled out onto Queen Street and fired into the early morning air. It was a relatively harmless operation. The quartermaster always saw to it that the charge wasn't big enough to make much more noise than a car backfiring.

But this morning there was no quartermaster on duty and so the C.O. decided to prepare the charge himself. And that would have been all right, too, except that several of the other officers, all soused, helped him with the job and kept saying, "That's not enough; put more in," and "I could fart a louder noise than that will make," and so on. And the C.O., who was anything but chicken, kept adding more powder and more wadding and stuffing it down into the shell casing.

56

Finally, as they say, all was in readiness, and with much saluting and aye-aye and sir-ing, the gun was hauled out into the street. It was then about four o'clock. It just so happened that four was the exact time the milkmen start out from the Excelsior Dairy two blocks down the street, with their wagons loaded with bottles of fresh, sweet milk and their horses frisky after resting and eating oats.

So we all lined up. Smiley and I by now had become buddies of everybody and rank was forgotten. Egheart approached the Captain in a manner which couldn't be described as "smartly," saluted similarly and said, "Enemy sighted off the starboard quarter, shur."

I'm not sure he meant the milkman's rig that was clip-clopping along, or if he was just speaking hypothetically. Anyway, the Captain returned the salute and shouted, "Prepare to fire!"

"Ready to fire, shur!"

"Fire!"

It was variously reported in the *Wabagoon Daily Sentinel* and the *Prairie Producer* and CKLS morning news that the sound that violated the peace of the morning was a bomb, a tremendous charge of dynamite, or a torpedo from a German sub that had somehow found its way up the Wabagoon River.

What it did waken was the milkman's horse, contentedly trotting along. This, I'm sure he thought, was the end that his mother had warned him would overtake him when his usefulness was finished. His ears and tail shot up simultaneously, fire shot out of his nostrils and he took off at something more than a gallop with the sleepy driver, also come to life, shouting and screaming. Around the corner came the wagon on two wheels, so that several full cases of bottled milk slid out the open side door, making a wild clatter on the pavement. Straight past us the wagon flew, bottles flying. Not able to turn the next corner, they tore right out over the CNR railway tracks, and when the wagon hit the first rails it shot straight up into the air, did a double somersault and landed on its back with the horse still going at full tilt.

Nobody investigated what happened after that. The

twelve pounder was quickly wheeled in through the side door, the door locked and barred, and the officers and their ladies repaired to the wardroom to continue their revels.

I was somewhat startled by it all and my eyes must have been popping out of my head, but Smiley, always calm, merely shook his head ruefully and muttered, "Children, that's what they are, just little children."

The ending of that memorable wardroom party was, for me, spectacular. When it came time to go home, most of the officers were, surprisingly, in good enough shape to drive themselves and each other through the deserted streets of Wabagoon to wherever they lived. All but Hotshot. And so it was that I was detailed to drive him and Miss Reilly home in the staff car.

Smiley and I carried the comatose Hotshot out the door and loaded him into the back seat, where he promptly fell over and began to snore. So there was no place for Miss Patricia Reilly to sit but up in the front seat with me.

Even after all these years I can still relive the thrill of having Patricia next to me. I was in a daze, on a cloud, in heaven, on the street where she lived and all the other phrases that have been used to describe a youth smitten by love. I know that I drove slowly and took the long, long route to Hotshot's house, where I had to pick him up bodily and carry him up his front steps. There was a couch on the porch, I remember, and it was a warm night, so I dumped him there and left.

"Will he be all right?" Patricia wanted to know when I got back in the car. She never asked me why I delivered him home before I delivered her, but I'm sure she wondered about it.

"Slightly hung over is all," I reassured her. "Naval officers have to be able to hold their liquor."

"Disgusting!" she snorted, and I left it at that.

Her house was only about two blocks away, but I managed to make a few wrong turns before getting there. When I stopped the car she said, "Thanks for the ride. What is your name?"

There it was. That damned name again. I gulped. "Diespecker. Ordinary Seaman Diespecker."

"But you must have another name."

"Yeah!" I couldn't tell her it was Dink, so I decided to come clean. "It's Robin."

"Robin." And so help me, from her lips it sounded great. "I like it. Has a nice sound. Robin."

"I'm beginning to like it now, too." I wanted her to stay in the car, although having her this close to me was somewhat uncomfortable. Old joke! "Why are a sailor's trousers like a small town hotel?" Answer! "Because there is no ballroom." There is also little room for anything else.

"Why do you say that? I mean, about liking your name now?" Patricia cooed.

"Well, uh, you know, because you like it."

"Does that mean you like me?"

"Well . . . yes."

"Then why don't you sit a little closer?" Whereupon she moved over against me. Then so help me she put her arm around my neck and pulled my head over and kissed me on the mouth. That did it. As we used to say, I almost burst my britches with excitement. I started to kiss her with some enthusiasm but she squirmed away, opened the door and jumped out.

"Good night, you darling, gallant sailor boy," I heard her say, but before I could get out of the car she was inside the house.

I drove back to the ship in somewhat of a daze. Things weren't so bad aboard old *Porpoise* after all.

6

For Those in Peril

"Wakie, wakie, rise and shine!"

Somebody was shaking my hammock roughly, so roughly that I tumbled out of it onto the cement deck of HMCS *Porpoise*.

"What the hell?" I mumbled sleepily, staring up into the grinning face of Chief Petty Officer Lightson. Funny thing, but even today when I'm jarred out of sleep by a loud noise or a grandchild pouncing on my ample stomach or my wife shaking me to stop my snoring, in the first moment of consciousness I half expect to see Lightson's face. Such was the traumatic effect he had on me; I had other bosses in the navy, plenty of them, but he was the first. And so lingers the effect of C.P.O. Lightson.

"Up and at 'em, Dees-pecker!" he bellowed. "Church Parade at ten hundred hours."

"Church what?"

"I guess it's too much for a heathen like you to understand, but this ship's company marches in a body to church every fourth Sunday. This is the day."

"But I just hit the sack! I was working."

"Oh yes, I heard all about that party. I guess everybody in the city heard of it. If I didn't know you were too stupid to manage it, I'd wager that you mixed up that extra heavy charge for the twelve pounder. Smartly, now. Get yourself dressed and this sleeping gear properly stowed. And mind you shave that ugly puss of yours."

As I staggered towards the seamen's head to do Lightson's bidding, I passed the Captain on his way aft to see the C.P.O. He looked so completely awful: glazed eyes, sallow face, and that look about the mouth that suggests a certain lack of control. Just looking at him made me feel better. He has to lead this parade into a church, I thought. Poor him.

When I came out of the heads, washed and shaved and showered, the first people I saw were Sam and Mike. Sam had a rather dazed look about him, like a man who'd undergone a traumatic experience. I later learned that he had. Lost his cherry to Gertie, the landlady's daughter. Mike was his usual voluble self.

"Where the hell were you all weekend? I phoned your house about four times, but your mother wouldn't say."

"Right here. Confined to barracks."

"Again? Tough. Boy, did you miss a time. We found a hoor house over on Regent Street. I never seen anything like it. I never even heard of anything like it. Four girls in the family and they're all hoors, starting from the youngest who's only fourteen."

"Sounds great. You probably got a dose."

"Not me. I had my navy issue to keep me clean." He flashed a package of condoms in front of my eyes. "They passed these out as we went ashore. This navy thinks of everything."

"How did you make out, Sam?" I asked.

"What? Oh, fine. Just great."

"Sam ain't talking about what he did," Mike confided from the corner of his mouth. "Probably went to see a Shirley Temple movie."

The bosun piped Fall In then and we all fell into our respective platoons, were right dressed, numbered, yelled at, inspected by leading seamen. Leading Seaman Yorny, who was in charge of our platoon, paused in front of me.

"Well, Diespecker, aren't you doing well for your first week in the navy?" It wasn't said unkindly, rather with a sense of awe. "I've known guys get into shit in a hurry, but you take the cake." Then he passed on as other ratings cast half-admiring glances my way. I was becoming bloody famous.

Lightson made a little speech. "Now listen, when we are out on the street, it's the navy on parade. The senior service. So let's have those heads up and those arms swinging to show the citizens how proud we are to be in His Majesty's senior service!"

Then he barked out the orders that marched us out onto the street in front of the barracks. A couple of old ladies and three kids paused in their morning activities to stand on the sidewalk and watch. The officers came out and each platoon was handed over to an officer. The ones who hadn't been at the party marched smartly to their positions. The others tried to, with varying degrees of success.

Then we marched. Of all the things I did in the navy I liked marching best. Striding along in the crisp morning air, arms swinging from the shoulder, everybody in step, heads up, chests out, great. *Porpoise*, of course, didn't boast a band, but the Sea Cadets had a drum and bugle band that led us down the street.

We marched down Regal Avenue, then down Princess Street and along River Crescent. Here the street was filled with churchgoers and they paused to watch us march past. Some smiled, others clapped their hands lightly, and some older men, veterans of other wars, came smartly to attention and gave us a salute. Our steps became brisker, our backs straighter, our arms stiffer and we realized what Lightson had meant. Representatives of His Majesty's Navy were we. Nelson's Navy, by God!

And then we came to Charles Wesley United Church. This was a switch, I realized later. Usually the navy marched to an Anglican Church, which was the established church of the navy as it was of Britain. But the United Church people of Wabagoon had complained of this and hence this special parade to the Charles Wesley. Considering the conditions of the officers and the gossip running around town, we'd have been far better off to have been on our way into the Anglican church.

The Charles Wesley was the largest and most prestigious United church in the city. It was an imposing sight, constructed of grey stone with two square towers and huge, beautifully etched front windows. Before church union, it had been a Methodist church and it still retained many of the sterner aspects of that stern sect. Particularly was this true of the current minister, the Reverend August Brown, who could curl the soul of a sinner with a glance.

So we marched up the wide stone steps and through the wide front doors and down the hushed aisles to the special section, dead front and centre, that had been reserved for us. From where I sat I could see the back of the Captain's head with the red neck and bristles of his fresh haircut. It seemed to me it wavered ever so slightly and had to be jerked back into place, as though its owner had momentarily dozed off.

The huge pipe organ was quietly droning the navy hymn, "Eternal Father Strong to Save." In front of the organ sat the choir in their black gowns with white collars, and in front of them the three altars from which Reverend Brown would do his stuff.

It turned out we'd been a little late getting there and so the proceedings began at once. And one of the first things on the agenda was the reading of the lesson. And that privilege, I was shocked to realize, was to be enjoyed by our Captain. How in the world, I wondered, is he going to make it to the front in his delicate condition, and read that lesson without disaster striking?

I don't suppose in his naval career, and it turned out to be quite a career, did Lieutenant Gridley face a situation more fraught with rue than this very one. Every eye in the vast cavern of Charles Wesley United Church was fixed on him, and included among them were some of the sternest eyes in Wabagoon.

He was sitting on an aisle seat. I could feel him measuring

the distance between himself and the pulpit, counting the steps as a condemned man must count the steps to the gallows.

Very carefully he rose to his feet and stood in the aisle as though testing the capacity of his legs to hold him up. Then, stiff as a board, he began the slow march to the front. Every eye followed him, except those of the officers in the rows ahead of me. Their heads were bowed, I suppose in prayer that their leader would make it.

Slowly and deliberately, and oh so carefully, this representative of Nelson's Navy marched down that aisle, with great deliberation and care navigated the three steps up to the pulpit level, wavered slightly and then, manoeuvring himself into position, clutched the sides of the pulpit top in the manner of a preacher about to deliver eternal truths.

I saw his head jerk back ever so slightly as he focused his eyes on the print of the huge Bible before him. Then he began to read.

"Wine is a mocker, strong drink a brawler and whoever is led astray by it is not wise."

Once he almost faltered. His head bent forward slightly and sweat glistened on his brow.

"My God," I heard somebody in front of me whisper, "he's going to pass out!"

And it was then that his naval training came to the fore. All those lectures and boxing matches and long duty watches at Cornwallis paid off. Steadfastness under fire, that was it. The knuckles of his hands were white, sweat ran down the side of his nose in little rivulets. The congregation held its collective breath.

"May God bless the reading of this, His word."

He'd made it. A sweet smile covered his flushed face as he raised it to face the congregation. Deliberately, he closed the Holy Book before him and, stiff and straight, navigated the necessary steps back to his seat on the aisle. Very gently he lowered his head to his hand and I could feel the approval of the good churchgoers in the seats nearby as they watched their hero, overcome with emotion, in a moment of silent meditation and prayer.

The choir stood up and sang the navy hymn, the same hymn the ship's company stumbled through every morning, but with this choir singing it, it sounded good.

And then came the sermon.

Reverend Brown was built, as we were wont to say in the navy, like a brick outhouse. Solid, that was the word for Brown. Solid body, solid head, which sat on his square shoulders without any sign of a neck and was covered with a mass of wild black hair, and a solid mind.

He was a preacher of the old school. No nonsense. No compromise with evil. His wide mouth was a straight line beneath his straight, sharp nose.

He stepped up to the pulpit, clutched the sides as our beloved captain had done just moments before, and gazed over our heads at the great stained glass windows featuring beautiful pictures of Christ among the Elders, as though seeking inspiration, and then he began to talk.

"We are engaged in a war that surely epitomizes more than any war at any time the eternal struggle between good and evil. We did not ask for this war. We did not want it. But there comes a time when righteous men must stand up to the Devil and say, 'Stop! You have gone so far and you will go no farther!'

"As I look down on the faces of these young men in front of me, I'm filled with sorrow and humility. Some so young they've scarce had time to live, to know the love of a good woman, to feel the touch of their child's fingers upon their cheek, and we are making them go and fight and, yes, die for us."

He paused and glared down at the businessmen before him. "Yes, we are asking them to go and protect us. And I ask you, what have we done for them? These are the same young men that a year or so ago we were calling bums. Whom we turned from our doors and our places of business because we had no use for them. No use at all! The same boys! Are you not ashamed that now in our fear and distress we call upon them and say, 'Help us! Protect us! Give up your youth and possibly your lives that we may be safe!' "

The dark eyes beneath the immense black brows burned with a menacing fire. "Yes, asking them to give up their young manhood. To leave their homes and their schools and their loved ones to face the enemies' bullets and torpedoes, and giant shells that can blow a small corvette out of the water with no trace left. And besides the torpedoes and bullets and bombs, we ask them to face something that is far worse."

Everybody leaned forward to learn what could be worse than torpedoes, bullets, and bombs.

"Sin! That is what we are asking them to face! The sin that goes with military service. Drinking and fornicating and carousing, aye, and killing. All these are sins. And the worst of these is *drink*!"

I could feel the officers shrinking down in their seats. And from somewhere in about the middle of a row came the distinct sound of a deep snore. It was Sub-Lieutenant Hotshot who, prematurely dragged from his bed, was peacefully sleeping off the effects of last night's party. Somebody planted an elbow in his ribs and he came to with a jerk.

Reverend Brown was warming up to his favourite theme. He had an audience filled with the kind of remorse and guilt that can come only with a fiendish hangover, and he knew it.

"Yes, I say that of all the enemies you young men will face, alcohol is the most fiendish, the most hateful, the most seductive of all. It will be thrust at you from every side. The manufacturers of those poisons masquerading under the names of beer and wine and hard liquor are rubbing their hands with glee and stepping up production an hundredfold. They are lying in wait for you at every turn. On every page of your newspapers and magazines you'll find advertising equating the drinking of these foul brews with the good life. Yes, and on billboards on the very streets. In your canteen. Everywhere you look you will see the demon alcohol!"

I don't know about the others, but this was making me decidedly thirsty.

The sermon ended as abruptly as it had begun, and Reverend Brown led the congregation in prayer for our protection from the torpedoes and bullets and bombs and sin. It was a long prayer and some of the officers in the row ahead of me had to be jostled awake when it was finished.

And then when we got up to go I received a considerable shock. Sitting in the aisle seat directly across from me was Patricia. She'd been there all the time and I hadn't known it. A good thing, I suppose, because had I known it I'd have spent the entire time staring at her. As I stood up she gave me the slightest smile, such as any pretty girl might bestow on a sailor who is going out to risk torpedoes and bullets and bombs and sin. I couldn't know for sure. I paused and smiled at her, but somebody nudged me from behind and I marched down the aisle to the big doors.

We mustered outside the church before the admiring eyes of the congregation and got ready to march back to the ship. The pace from church, I thought, was brisker than it had been on the way to church. Like a horse returning to the barn for a feed of oats.

Only in this instance the officers were returning to the wardroom. They practically ran us down the street, paying little attention to whether we were in step or not. Smiley was in for a busy day.

The ship's company was dismissed. The others went hence from there to enjoy the remainder of their weekend. And I went back to my hammock for the first long, uninterrupted sleep I'd had since joining HMCS *Porpoise*.

I dreamed about Patricia.

7

Pay Parade

"Diespecker, R.E.F."

My name was called out for my first navy pay. I'd been standing in line for most of an hour, slowly inching forward towards the table where the paymaster and a couple of his writers sat with a pile of money in front of them. The ship's company of HMCS *Porpoise* was being paid off.

I had finally served out all my punishment time and had been allowed to go home - pardon me, ashore - nights. My family was glad to see me. Mother, of course, had been somewhat confused about the whole thing.

"Why couldn't you come home before?" she had asked, wrinkling her forehead.

"Because I had Number Eleven."

She frowned. Numbers One and Two had long been used in our family for going to the bathroom, but Number Eleven was just plain ridiculous.

"It's a form of punishment," I explained, realizing that this would worry her even more.

"Punishment? Robin, did you do Something Bad?"

"Well, it's nothing serious, actually. You know when you first get into the navy it's easy to break little rules."

"But, Robin, you shouldn't break rules; you know that."

"I can tell you, Ma, it doesn't mean a damned thing."

"Well, I don't know. And there's no need to swear about it, I'm sure."

Then she was off on another tack. When I'd been in high school and learning all about the evils of war and how the world had to have peace at all cost, I had become pretty sophisticated in my ideas about the first war, which Ma remembered with horror.

I would say things like, "Wars are just the result of greed and avarice and the desire to exploit on the part of all nations."

And she would answer, "That's nonsense. Everybody knows that it was the Germans who started the war. That hateful Kaiser Bill."

"The Germans were no worse than anybody else," I'd explain patiently.

"How can you say such a thing? After all those wicked things they did in Belgium to helpless women and children! I've seen pictures!"

"Everybody's seen those lurid pictures of soldiers bayonetting babies and so on. All fakes. Germans wouldn't kill children any more than we would."

By that time she'd be close to tears. "Really, Robin, I don't know where you get such ideas. If you'd been alive then and read the papers."

All of which proved to me then how antiquated and prejudiced my mother was in her thinking. The more I tried to explain to her the intricacies of international relations, as I'd mastered them in Grade Twelve at Patuna Collegiate, the more upset she became. And now she felt that what the Germans were doing to England and the Fifth Columnists they'd used in Denmark and Norway to take over those countries proved her point conclusively.

Every afternoon she read the war news in the *Wabagoon Sentinel* and each night listened to Lorne Greene, the Voice of Doom, telling us what had happened. And she listened religiously to the propaganda plays, such as *Nazi Eyes Over Canada*, which featured our own brand of Fifth Columnists and spelled out the horrible tortures and mutilations that would be our lot if the Germans won the war. And so she was convinced her worst fears had been justified.

The bombing of British cities that summer particularly bothered her. For she'd been raised on the idea that Britain ruled the waves and the air and everything else worth ruling. She sat by the radio listening to the reports of the Battle of Britain and those great speeches of Churchill and, like people over there, she never once doubted that the British would prevail. She'd been right all along.

And while the British airmen fought the Battle of Britain, I had fought the battle of HMCS *Porpoise*. We learned a few things that helped us later on. Bends and hitches and knots and splices I loved. For this purpose Harry Binns had constructed a twenty-foot square with four posts on heavy metal bases, a line joining the posts. The class of sailors stood around the outside of this square, each with a three-foot length of rope with which we practised our bends and hitches on the heavy line in front of us. The instructor was in the middle, walking from man to man inspecting our efforts and saying things like, "No, not that way. I told you, for a bowline it's 'The rabbit comes up the hole, around the tree, and down the hole again.' See. Like this. Up through there, around here and down again. Try it again."

Up until then the only two knots I could tie right were a reef knot and a slip knot; now I learned the others and have never forgotten them. And splices. I'd seen and admired them before, and had even made some abortive attempts to master them. Now under Binns' patient tutelage I learned the long splice and the short splice and the eye splice, and to this day when I've nothing better to do I'll sit down and splice a couple of rope ends together.

Morse code had been pretty easy. I took my seamanship manual home and rigged up a little key and Doug and I practised together in the evenings. We did the same with semaphore flags and the cards they gave us for the identification of silhouettes of Axis Nations' warships. The more I learned the more anxious I got to get away from HMCS *Porpoise*

70

and off to sea. I kept a careful record of each day that passed until my six-week stint would be up, and I would go to help fight the Battle of the North Atlantic.

But there was always Chief Petty Officer Lightson. It seemed to me that he went out of his way to berate, ridicule, bully, and humiliate me. On the advice of Smiley, I took it all. "You can't fight back in the navy," Smiley warned. "You just got to take it. Who knows, maybe he'll get to love you."

"Heaven forbid."

So I took it, pretty well, until pay parade.

We all lined up and as we stepped up to receive our money we saluted smartly, executed the naval manoeuvre known as Off Caps, stated our names, rating and numbers and, holding our round caps out, received our pay on the tops of them. It was more money than I'd seen in a long time. My regular two dollars per day, plus the living-out allowance. I stuffed it into my pocket and, along with Sam and Mike, began to plan an expedition to the Imperial Hotel beverage room, where we'd find out just how much beer we could consume in an evening and still make it home.

We'd learned that on pay day the ship's company was usually dismissed at four o'clock to give the ratings time to pay their landladies and so on, or more likely, just because it was pay day.

Four o'clock came and we were mustered on the main deck where we restlessly waited to be dismissed. But we weren't dismissed. Something was definitely wrong. Lightson had a grim look on his sharp face and the leading hands looked worried. We stood there and stood there and finally the Captain came out through the office door, marched across the floor and stood in front of us.

"Men, I really hate to say what I'm about to say. One man has reported that his entire pay has been stolen."

A shudder ran through the ranks.

The Captain waited a moment for this to sink in and then continued. "Of all the crimes that a man can commit in the navy, thievery is the worst. We live in such close quarters on board ship that we must be able to trust each other implicitly.

71

Now this is not a clear-cut case of thievery. The man whose pay has been stolen knows that he put the money in his wallet and put the wallet in his dickey, and now the wallet is gone. It may have fallen out of his dickey and somebody may have picked it up with the idea of finders keepers. If that's the case, we are going to give that man a chance to return the money. He can simply leave it on a table, any table, when nobody is looking and it will be found. So Chief Petty Officer Lightson will have you fall out for fifteen minutes. In that time I hope the wallet will be returned and no questions will be asked."

So we fell out and milled around the barracks self-consciously, but nobody placed any wallet on any table.

We were mustered again, and again the Captain spoke to us. "All right, men. This now is a case of thievery. We know that nobody has left the ship since pay parade and nobody has come in. So the thief and the money are still here. And nobody will leave this ship until the money is found."

He turned and walked away and the other officers followed him into the front part of the ship. Then Lightson took over. He stood in front of us without saying anything and then, looking squarely at me, he began.

"There is one man here who is fouling things up for everybody else. If you know who he is, don't be fool enough to protect him, because he's not worth protecting. Because of him, you are all going to stay aboard this ship until that wallet is found. If it takes a week or a month, nobody leaves here until the money is returned. So it's up to each one of you to help find the thief. Dismiss."

So we wandered around the place, feeling as though we were somehow implicated in a crime, somehow guilty ourselves. Somebody among us was a thief.

After about half an hour of this aimless wandering and sitting and not talking much to anyone, the officers came out of the wardroom in a group and we were ordered to fall in again. Then each man was required to open his locker and all the lockers were thoroughly searched by officers.

Nothing.

The next step was to search all the ratings. This, we were

informed, would be done by the officers.

"What if it's one of the officers who pinched the pay?" Mike whispered as we were waiting for this final search.

"What?" Sam's big face was furrowed with concern. "Gosh, an officer'd never do a thing like that."

"Why not?"

"Well, you know. Shucks, they're officers."

And so they went to work on us. Each officer had a group of sailors to work with and we took turns. Every stitch of clothing had to come off and be searched. Underwear, socks, right down to their stinking toes, shoes, everything.

This was a terrible ordeal for me. When confronted by a situation such as this, I immediately feel guilty. It must be my Methodist upbringing or the influence of my mother, or maybe just that I'm a nut, but my first reaction to any situation is somehow that I'm to blame.

Besides this, I would invariably be beset with an even worse condition, known in our family as "the trots" or "the sliders," which in plain language meant a complete and horrifying inability to control my bowels, so that I had to go to the bathroom often and quickly.

So as I stood in line, fidgeting and sweating and heaving my weight from one foot to the other, I gave every indication of being guilty as hell. Worse, I was sure that Lightson was, as they say, keeping his eye on me. He stood off about twenty feet, hands locked behind him, feet slightly apart, staring at me. He'd already undergone his search, a humiliating experience for a C.P.O., and this made him more determined that when the thief was caught no mercy would be shown.

As I drew closer to my searcher, young Sub-Lieutenant Washingham, who was still wet behind the ears and, to make matters worse, from Toronto, and the stale odour of rotting socks assailed my nostrils, my guilt manifestations became extreme. I dared not look at Lightson, and my attempts to avoid his eye made me even more conspicuous.

Young Washingham, I'm sure, was appalled at what he was seeing as he searched these prairie lads fresh from the Depression. He came from a background where a shower every evening and maybe one in the morning to boot was mandatory. Here on the prairie with the drought that had cursed us for ten years, we'd got into the habit of bathing maybe once a week. And some of these lads from the southern part of the province where the drought had been most extreme probably took their weekly bath in water that had already removed the dirt from three or four other siblings.

Now it was my turn, and now the curse was upon me. I looking appealingly at the sub-lieutenant with his natty blue serge suit and oh so white shirt and carefully shined half-Wellingtons, and I felt like Oliver Twist before the beedle.

"Please, sir," I said, "I have to go."

"What? Go where, my man? You know that no one can leave the ship."

"I don't have to leave the ship; I just have to go big pots."

I realized what I'd done. In my nervousness a childhood synonym for bowel movement had sprung into my mind.

"What are you talking about?" the bewildered subbie asked.

"I have to go to the head."

"To the head? Now?" I looked so miserable and so guilty that I'm sure he thought this was some sort of ruse to get rid of incriminating evidence. "Impossible!"

"If I don't I'll shit my pants!"

That did it. The prospect of having to search through my underwear after such an accident was too much for him.

"Very well, then," he barked. "On the double."

If ever an order was redundant that was one. On the double my eye. I made it to the heads on the triple or maybe even the quadruple. But I made it, and just in time.

When I got up and pushed the button to flush the toilet nothing happened. I pushed it again and still nothing happened. I lifted the top off the tank and peered down into the rusty water and found the trouble. Something black and flat was jammed in between the lever and the side of the box. I fished in with my hand and pulled out a soggy billfold. The stolen money! The thief had obviously panicked when the search was announced and dumped his loot.

What to do? Leave it there? No, after the search the thief would simply go back and get it. The heads had already been thoroughly searched and so probably wouldn't be again. But if I turned it in . . . what then?

I made up my mind quickly. Holding the dripping wallet in my outstretched hand I went out of the heads, across the drill floor straight to Sub-Lieutenant Washingham and presented it to him. "Found this in the toilet tank, sir."

"What's this? The stolen wallet!" He grabbed it, made a brisk right turn and marched over to where the Captain was standing and handed it to him. The Captain opened it, inspected it, heaved a sigh of relief. For a moment I felt like a hero, until I felt a hand on my shoulder.

"Pretty damned smart, Dees-pecker," a voice hissed. It was Lightson.

"What? What do you mean?"

"Oh come on! That's an old trick. Pretending you had to shit and then dumping the wallet."

"But I did have to go!" I was in a spot and I knew it. Then I remembered something. "Permission to see the Captain!"

"Damned right. Come with me." So he marched me over to where a little group of officers had gathered.

"Sir!" I shouted when we got close, before Lightson could say anything.

"What is it, Diespecker?"

"Well, Chief Petty Officer Lightson says that I went to the heads to dump that wallet. That I didn't have to go at all. I can prove that I did if you'll come with me, sir!"

"I'll take care of this –" Lightson began.

"No, I'll go with him. Lead on."

I led the way to the heads and pointed into the bowl, and there was ample proof that at least I'd had to go.

The Captain made a face and said nothing. Turned and walked away.

Right away we were mustered and the Captain said, "The missing wallet has been found, intact, with all the money in it, and no more questions will be asked. Dismissed."

And so ended my first pay parade in the navy.

8

What You Get
Is Sweet Fanny Apples

"When both lights you see ahead
Starboard wheel and show your red.
Green to green, red to red,
Perfect safety, go ahead."

We were all sitting in the recreation room, or slouching would
be a better word, while Lightson gave us his favourite lecture.
Rules of the Road. We'd been going over them and over them
and now we were supposed to have memorized all the little
verses that helped fix them in the mind, as Lightson said.
Lightson loved those little rhymes. A regular Thomas Gray he
was.

"All right, you, Dees-pecker," he snapped. "All ships must
keep a look-out, and steamships must stop and go astern if
necessary."

This was my cue to leap to attention and recite:

"Both in safety and in doubt
Always keep a good look-out.
In danger with no room to turn,
Ease her – stop her – go astern."

But I'd just got smartly to my feet and opened my mouth when that damned Mike, who was next to me, whispered in a voice that only I could hear:

"When in danger, when in doubt,
Run in circles, scream and shout!"

And sure enough, that's what came out of my mouth.

It was the nervousness, I suppose. It was getting so that every time I got close to Lightson I made some kind of dumb move just from pure funk. I had a teacher like that in school once, a Latin teacher of whom I was completely terrified. And certainly Lightson was bringing out the worst in me.

Now he just looked at me as though I was something that had crawled out of the bilge of a very dirty ship.

"One thing the navy doesn't need is a smart ass. Grab that rifle and do twenty laps around the deck. On the double!"

As I plodded about the hot deck with aching arms and legs, I again went through my calculations. This was an estimate of the number of hours that I would have to put up with Lightson before I was drafted out of there. The length of our stay in HMCS *Porpoise* was six weeks. I had already put in three weeks and two days and, when I finished this stint around the deck, approximately four and a half hours. This would leave me exactly two weeks, four days, nineteen hours and thirty minutes before that great day when I'd take the train for St. Hyacinthe Naval Base in Quebec. St. Hyacinthe, which until then I'd never even heard of, had become the magic word to me.

Apart from Lightson, I was rather enjoying my training at *Porpoise*. Especially the days we spent on the river learning boat-pulling. Binns was our instructor and he was perfect.

"Oars Ready!" he'd shout from his position in the stern, facing us. "Now lads, put your backs to it, and remember straight back, arms straight when swinging back, hands dropped before the wrists to ensure the blade clearing the water, legs driving from the stretcher as soon as the body takes the strain. Now, all together. One. Two. Three. Four. Toss!"

And away we'd go up the river against the current, underneath the Crescent Street Bridge in the summer sunlight, with a group of small boys running along the bank shouting out a repeat of all Binns' orders, and reminding me of when I was that age myself and playing along that same river bank.

And then, later, there was the gun drill where we took the twelve pounder all apart and loaded it in the whaler and rowed across the river, leapt ashore, rushed up the bank with the barrel and the wheels and other parts and put them all together, with Binns timing us on his stop watch. Precision, that was the thing. On special occasions when we got real good at it, we'd put on demonstrations for the Wabagoon citizens, who stood in little groups wondering perhaps in what possible way such a drill and such a gun could keep Hitler's landing barges from invading Britain. I used to wonder about that myself.

And heaving the lead. That was the most fun of all. That is, it was until we had the accident.

The hand lead and line is used to tell the depth of water. It consists of a fourteen-pound lead weight at the end of twenty-five fathoms of a one-and-one-eighth-inch line. Of course it is done from the deck of a ship, but since we had no ship Binns had rigged up a twelve-foot tower on the railway property across the street from *Porpoise*. The leadsman would stand on a platform at the top and heave the lead, a manoeuvre accomplished by letting it swing back and forth like a pendulum a couple of times and then swinging it around over his head in a complete circle and letting it go forward. Then he called out the depth from different coloured pieces of bunting spliced into the line. White for five fathoms, red for seven, blue for thirteen and so on. "By the mark, five! By the mark, fifteen!"

It was good fun. We took turns climbing up to the platform and swinging the lead in great perpendicular circles and letting it go into a straight line along the side of the railway track. You had to remember a few things like coiling your rope so it didn't get kinky, and, of course, letting go of the rope at the right moment so that the fourteen-pound weight didn't pull you off the tower. The men who weren't heaving held the legs of the wooden tower so that it wouldn't fall over.

Everybody got the hang of it pretty quickly, except Sam. He had such incredible strength in those long arms of his, gained from many hours of hard farm work, that he was reluctant to let go the rope. While to the rest of us swinging that lead above our heads took considerable effort, Sam twirled it around like a kid making a yo-yo go around the world. As a result, he held back and let the thing drop a few feet in front of the tower.

"You've got to heave it, lad," Binns explained patiently. "Really give it a big swing and then, just before it reaches the horizontal, let it go. Don't be afraid of it. Give it a big heave!"

But Sam was still reluctant, giving it those tentative little thrusts that let the lead fall limply into the weeds below, until, for the one and only time in all the period I knew him, Petty Officer Binns lost his temper.

"For Christ sake, lad, *heave the damned thing!*"

Unfortunately, this exhortation came at the exact moment that the lead was descending from its highest point and when a CNR yard engine happened to be puffing along the track. Sam lost his temper, too, I guess, and heaved the line with such force that the holders of the tower legs were taken off guard and couldn't keep it upright. It leaned forward precariously, causing Sam to get slightly off target with his swing so that the surprised engineer, sitting by the open window of the cab, suddenly found himself with a fourteen-pound weight in his lap. All of which resulted in the loss of one lead and line and an angry letter from the CNR requiring *Porpoise* to remove its tower from railway property.

Sam was the pitcher of our softball team, and softball was the recreation that kept me sane.

Every kid in the prairies plays baseball or softball from the time he can walk, and I was no exception. Before all the snow was off the ground in spring, we'd be out playing catch, throwing the ball back and forth endlessly, listening to the smack in the glove, feeling the tingle on the palm of the hand, stretching the arm and just plain feeling good.

And then as the spring advanced and the diamonds dried

out, we'd pick up teams or play one-o-cat, endlessly catching, pitching, batting, running, arguing. Nothing organized; no umpire; just a bunch of neighbourhood kids disputing each close decision but somehow managing to get through the game. Then we got into organized softball on the public school teams and high-school teams. It was never called "fastball," as it is now, always "softball," although the ball was as hard as a rock. On our high-school team only the catcher and first baseman wore gloves; the rest played barehanded.

From the beginning I had been catcher. Standing behind the plate, digging fastballs out of the dirt, having foul tips bounce off every part of my anatomy, a receiver. Matter of fact, that's what I've been in life, a receiver rather than a disher-outer. In hockey I naturally played goal.

Anyway, we had a whiz of a softball team. Sam, for all his seemingly ponderous ways, could pitch a softball with the speed and accuracy of a rifle shot. His only problem was that he wanted to pitch every game, regardless of how many we played in a day. Mike played shortstop with speed and dexterity and the grace of a ballet dancer. The other players were equally good and enthusiastic. Sub-Lieutenant Egheart managed to get some money from the wardroom contingency fund to outfit us with uniforms, a V-neck jersey and long pants with a blue stripe down the side of each leg. Best of all, we had the HMCS *Porpoise* crest - white with a blue border, a loose replica of the navy cap badge at the top and a leaping porpoise in the centre. We were a great-looking team.

Egheart's coaching, however, did little to dispel a long-held notion of mine that most coaches are superfluous. In the first place he knew nothing whatsoever about the game. At Upper Canada College he'd played soccer and cricket, and although it was difficult for me to comprehend a fellow Canadian who had never played either baseball or softball, such was the case. His coaching consisted entirely of standing on the sideline somewhere between third and home bases shouting words of encouragement right out of Kipling.

"That's it, chaps, play up, play up!" he'd yell when they had a man on base with none out. Or "Good show" when a player had fielded a ball and caught the runner at first.

Once he yelled, "Jolly well pitched," at Sam who in complete bewilderment called for time out and went over to ask him what he meant.

But his biggest gaff came during the first playoff game with the air force. They were in the field for the first inning and Sam was ready to pitch the first ball when Egheart suddenly started waving his arms and shouting, "Hold up, there, hold up!" and running towards the home plate umpire. The umpire called time and politely asked what the trouble was.

"I believe they have too many players on their team!" Egheart announced.

"What? I count only nine."

"No, no, that chap out there behind the second sack." He pointed to the second base umpire.

For most games we didn't have a second base umpire or for that matter one for first or third. But since this was a playoff, the league was splurging a bit.

Unfortunately the plate umpire, a huge man who'd been working games in Wabagoon for as long as I could remember, couldn't conceive of such ignorance and thought Egheart was pulling his leg, and he didn't appreciate leg-pulling.

"You're out of the game!" he roared.

I quickly explained the situation to him and he permitted our coach to remain, which made absolutely no difference to the game, which we won in extra innings.

After each game Sam and Mike and I would repair to the Imperial Hotel beverage room and relive the ballgame and generally assess our lives in the navy.

On one of these occasions, after a game in which Sam had been uncharacteristically ineffective as a pitcher and had been removed from the mound in the fourth inning after they'd got five runs off him, Mike was not in a good mood.

"What in hell happened to you out there anyway?"

"What? Sorry, I didn't catch what you said," Sam replied vaguely.

"That's what I mean. You're not with it. What's wrong? You can tell us."

"It's nothing."

"Bullshit it's nothing. Come on, out with it."

"Well, it's Gertie. She – "

"I might have knew. Chasey la fam."

"What?"

"French for 'There's always some gawdamned woman fouling up the works.' What's with Gert?"

"She wants us to get married."

"What? Are you off your nut?"

"Well, you see, we . . . well . . ."

"So you stuck it into her. Big deal. Yer not the first – "

He didn't finish. Sam leaped to his feet, placed a big paw on Mike's chest, gathering the heavy cloth of his jersey into his fist, and lifted his friend out of his chair. The other great fist was cocked ready to knock Mike's head off his shoulders and send it like a bowling ball bouncing along the floor, but I managed to catch the arm and hold it back.

"Sam!" I shouted. "For God sake!" But he didn't hear me. His face had gone completely white, his eyes were closed to narrow slits and he was a madman. I threw both arms around him and hauled back, but he shrugged me off, in the process knocking over the table and two chairs.

Mike squirmed from his grasp and grabbed him around the legs. By this time the waiter, who weighed about two hundred and fifty and was an ex-lineman from the Winnipeg Blue Bombers, had hurried to the scene and thrown a big arm around Sam's neck, effectively choking him. Even at that it took two more waiters to subdue him and get him out of there. Fortunately, no member of the shore patrol was in sight.

On the street he had calmed down enough to leave Mike alone, but not enough for conversation. Instead, he stomped off down the street, still white with rage.

"What in hell is with that guy?" Mike asked, trying to straighten his jersey and picking his cap from the sidewalk.

"I don't know. Never saw him like that before. But if I were you I'd make no more cracks about Gertie."

"You'd better believe it. And that damned broad probably just wants his allowance money. I bet any money."

"Bet, but don't say it."

"But we got to save him. Jeez, Dink, if he marries her and then finds out she's fooling around. Well, you saw what happened!"

"I saw what happened. And I agree. But there's absolutely nothing we can do to stop it. He'll kill the first man that says a word against Gert."

"Don't I know it. He'd a killed me if he'd ever let that haymaker go."

The next day Sam apologized to Mike, but nothing more was said about Gertie.

So the time dragged by. And then one morning the draft lists were posted on the notice board. This is what we'd all been waiting for. In six weeks we'd changed from farm boys, mechanics, bookkeepers, students, salesmen, carpenters, bricklayers or whatever into sailors. We'd become accustomed to our uniforms, learned the proper naval salute, become proficient in bends and hitches, learned how to march, slope arms, present arms, how to call the floors decks and walls bulkheads, and not to argue with anyone with more garbage on his sleeve than we had. In short, we'd picked up all the elementary accoutrements of sailoring.

We were ready, nay eager, nay frantic, to move on to the next stage of our training.

As the day of the list approached, excitement ran high around the deck of HMCS *Porpoise*. Most of us were leaving the prairies for the first time. The words St. Hyacinthe, Digby, Cornwallis and Newfie had become magic in our ears. Returning sailors talked of them knowingly. Everybody who'd ever been to Newfoundland beguiled us with "Stay where yer to, By, and I'll come to where yer at." Other sailors who'd already been to sea had told us about life aboard a corvette. "Those tubs roll in a heavy dew." We were ready for it all.

And then there was embarkation leave and, best of all, the giant embarkation party. Short as its history was, HMCS *Porpoise* had already developed traditions, and the finest of these was the embarkation party. Stories of how drunk ratings had got at these parties were legend. There was the time

Leading Seaman Yaks pissed in the coffee, the time the C.O. slipped on his ass in the middle of the dance floor. It was tradition for ratings and officers to fraternize, oblivious of the ensignia on sleeves, and get roaring drunk together. At the end of the party, the draft would line up in a drunken formation, get their farewell speech from the tipsy C.O. and then march down Regal Avenue, shouting and singing, to the CN station to be hauled away to fight the foe.

Everybody knew the exact day the draft list would be posted and on that day I came aboard an hour early, briskly saluted the quarterdeck and headed for the notice board. But Smiley, who had come aboard even earlier and was obviously waiting for me, yelled, "Hey, Dink, what's your hurry?"

"Out of my way, friend. I want to see that list."

"What's so important about the list? You in a great hurry to leave us?"

"You slobbered a bibful."

"Why? This isn't such a bad place."

Then I noticed that something was wrong. Smiley's long horse face was furrowed with concern.

"What in hell are you trying to tell me?"

"Take it easy, Dink."

"Take it easy my foot!" I tore over to the notice board and read the names, neatly typed in alphabetical order. Dabrowski, R. N., Dalton, E. S., Dinsmore. Something was wrong. There should be a name between Dalton and Dinsmore and it should be Diespecker, R. E. F.

I wasn't on the list!

I banged on the door of Chief Petty Officer Lightson's office, which was right beside the notice board. A calm voice sang out, "Enter."

Lightson was sitting behind his desk working away at something. He looked up and smiled his sweet smile.

"Yes?"

"I . . . I . . . I . . . I'm not on the draft list!"

"Deees-pecker, that bit of information hardly comes as a great surprise to me, since I made up the list."

"You mean it wasn't an accident? A mistake?"

"Certainly not. I rarely make such mistakes."

"But why? I passed all my tests. I did twice as well as some of those guys on the list. Why in the name of - "

"If you will just calm down a bit, I'll try to explain. Good. Now, you see it is the custom to hold over some of the better ratings of each ship's company to help with the new recruits. Monday we'll have sixty raw recruits who don't know a deck from a bulkhead, and need to be led by the hand, so to speak."

"Bullshit!"

Lightson's face went very red. He rose from his chair and leaned over the desk towards me.

"Yes, it is. The real reason is that you aren't ready to go. Oh, you got high marks in your semaphore and boat-pulling and the rest, but there's more to being a sailor than that, a hell of a lot more."

"What the hell do you mean?"

"I mean your attitude is all wrong. A sailor takes orders, see? He doesn't come busting in on a chief petty officer and shout at him. A good sailor respects his superiors."

"You bastard. I'm not taking this. I'll go to the C.O.!"

"You can go to the Admiral of the fleet if you want to, you cocky little prick, and it won't do you any good. The C.O. and I went over this list before it was posted. He agreed with me completely. Now get your ass out of here before I have you on report."

I don't know what I'd have done then. Probably ruined my naval career entirely and bought myself a court martial besides by striking a superior. But Smiley pushed open the door and stuck his head in and said, "Chief?"

"What the hell do you want?"

"Sorry. I didn't know you were busy."

"I'm not. Get out of here and take this, this, thing with you."

Before I could move Smiley grabbed me by the arm and, showing amazing strength, hauled me out the door and closed it.

"Jeees, Dink, what are you trying to do?"

I had to hit something. Couldn't hit Smiley. So I hit the bulkhead, but by that time some sense must have seeped into my head because I didn't hit it hard enough to break my hand.

"Come on, let's get the hell out of here," Smiley muttered and led me away. Soon after the boatswain piped Fall In and I was prevented from doing myself more damage.

I did manage to see the C.O., who was most sympathetic, promising to "look into" the situation. But the next day Smiley informed me that the C.O. himself had a new appointment, as had most of the junior officers including Egheart.

"Who else?" I inquired.

"Doc. Sure going to miss him. By the way, I'll need a couple of bucks from you."

"Huh?"

"Going away present for the C.O. and Doc."

Smiley was the self-appointed collector for presents for departing officers. There was nothing I could do but cough up.

"This is going to be some embarkation party," Smiley mused. "The officers have a farewell for the C.O. and the draft and all."

9

The Draft Party

"There is nothing in all this world that can match war for popularity. It is, to at least nine people out of ten, the supreme circus of circuses, the show beyond compare. It is Hollywood multiplied by ten thousand. It combines all the excitement of a bullfight, a revival, a train wreck, and a lynching. It is a hunt for public enemies with a million Dillingers scattered through the woods. It is the dizziest, gaudiest, grandest, damnest sort of bust that the human mind can imagine."

That's an excerpt from an article written by that scratchy old curmudgeon, H. L. Mencken, for *Liberty Magazine* in the issue of December 26, 1936. I've kept it around ever since I came across it when I was in high school.

I thought Mencken was crazy when, as a fuzz-faced idealist, I too thought war was finished. But when the war began I saw that everything that crotchety old cynic said was absolutely true.

And if we needed any further proof of the popularity of war, it was amply provided by the sense of excitement that ran through HMCS *Porpoise* on the eve of the draft party. Excitement? Hell, it was euphoria extreme, joy beyond compare.

We set about the job of making that dusty old garage fit to receive members of the public and to entertain them. We scrubbed and waxed and polished until the old place groaned beneath the weight of its respectability. The officers were no less excited; they loved a party as much as the rest of us.

The only people who weren't overcome by this grand and glorious feeling were the ones, like me, who weren't going. I was as mad as I've ever been about anything, mad enough to do something really drastic if the opportunity presented itself. My father sensed this, for he knew something of my terrible temper.

"Now, take it easy, Rob," he warned. "Look on the bright side. I know it's a big disappointment to you, but don't tempt fate. I remember a friend of mine who was disappointed because he couldn't get leave from the front line. A shell landed on the lorry that was taking those who had leave and killed them all. Those of us in the trenches weren't touched."

I wanted to shout "Bullshit!" at him, and to tell him to go to hell with his wise old saws and corny maxims. But I didn't. Mother was glad I'd missed the draft. She was certain, deep in her good Methodist soul, that I was sure to be killed or at least enticed into bad company and sinful action.

Doug was sympathetic, if confused. "When will you go?" he asked.

"Next draft in six weeks' time."

"What will you do until then?"

"Same thing I've been doing, I guess."

Mary was happy about it. She liked having a sailor about the house.

There was one person on the draft who was as doleful as I. That was Sam. He went around with a face - to quote Mike - long enough to eat oats out of the bottom of a churn. Sam and Gertie had been married the previous Saturday in a simple little ceremony at City Hall, attended only by the bride's mother.

At Stand Easy on Friday morning Mike and I found him brooding in a corner, brought him a chocolate bar and a coke and tried to buck him up.

"Cheer up, Sam," Mike urged, with his usual tact. "For chrissake this is a party, you know."

Sam didn't cheer up.

"Quit worrying about that . . . about Gertie. She'll . . . she'll . . ."

I took him by the arm and steered him away. "Come over here, there's something I want to show you."

When we were around the corner, Mike asked, "Whatsa idea?"

"You want to get your block knocked off, you dummy? Shut up about Gert!"

"Yeah, I guess so. But it makes me mad to think of that broad drawing Sam's allowance and half his pay, and gawd knows what she'll be doing."

"Cool it. Nothing we can do."

"Well, you'll be here. Keep an eye on her. Don't let her get away with nothing."

So much for Mike's understanding of marital relations, female psychology, and wartime brides. I didn't say any more. I'd just learned that I'd drawn quartermaster duty for the dance, which meant that while the others kicked up their heels with joy I would stand at the side door - excuse me, on the quarterdeck - keeping the log, banging off the time on the big brass bell, and fuming.

The worst of it was that I'd screwed up sufficient courage to ask Patricia to the dance two weeks before, and she'd showed considerable enthusiasm for the idea, confiding that she was sure Hotshot was going to ask her and she didn't want to go with him. So, I'd had to phone her and tell her that I was on duty and couldn't escort her. I didn't like the way she took it. Said something about her mother warning her never to trust a sailor, but there was something in her voice that wasn't joking.

I'd drawn the First Watch, which runs from 2000 to 0000 or, for you landlubbers, from eight in the evening until midnight. Since the dance would be over at eleven to leave time for the draft to march down to the station to catch the 11:30 train east, I wouldn't get a chance to dance with anybody.

Gad, how I did want to go on that train! I'd never slept on a train in my life. For that matter, I'd never ridden inside one for more than fifty miles except when I went harvesting the year I was in Grade Twelve.

And those lucky buggers were going to have two nights and three days on the train. Eating in the dining car, sleeping in upper and lower berths and, best of all, seeing something of the country. Seeing something besides the flat, flat prairies. Rivers and waterfalls and forests and big cities, and finally the sea.

I took up my post sharp at eight, and the first to arrive was none other than that sonofabitch Lightson. Oh, but he looked fine in his best uniform, and on his arm he had a beautiful brunette in a long dress with a daring cleft. He saluted the quarterdeck but didn't even look at me. Then he proceeded to lead his lady around his ship and show her all the things and places and dazzle her with his knowledge. I could hear her oh's and ah's and tinkling laughter as they went.

And I realized that every damned rating on the draft would be doing that with his girl, showing off, playing the great sailor man. The stupid buggers.

I was gazing into the recreation room and listening to this guff when somebody tapped me on the shoulder from behind. I turned and there was big Sam, wearing a sheepish grin on his face and Gertie on his arm.

Gertie! After all these years a clear picture of Gertie is etched on the microfilm of my memory. She was a big girl with blonde, fuzzy hair and blue eyes. But all this was overshadowed by her figure, which can best be described as Mae West-like. Her breasts were magnificent, pure white and bulging over the top of her purple peasant blouse. A small waist was pulled in by a broad cinch belt, topping a long green skirt with butterfly pleats that showed off her magnificent bottom. No doubt about it, the word for Gertie was magnificent.

"Uh, Dink," Sam was blushing more than somewhat. "I wantcha to meet my wife, Gertie. This here is Dink."

"Gosh. I'm sure glad to meet you, Gertie. Sam's talked a lot about you."

Gertie's blue eyes were cautious and a slight frown wrinkled her forehead. "Sam's talked a lot about you, too. Says you're his best friend." I had the distinct feeling that I was being analysed - undressed, more likely - by those big blue eyes. "Aren't you coming to the dance, Dink? Gawd, what a handle. You must have another."

I ignored that. "No, I'm on duty. Keeping a close lookout for enemy subs."

Gertie laughed loudly. Peered anxiously into the recreation room and pulled at Sam's arm. "Glad to have met you."

"Yeah. Me, too. Have a good time. Dance off both your shoes, Sam."

The big fellow grinned sheepishly and I sensed that he had little stomach for escorting his wife in among that gang of wolves. "Sure, Dink. Well, uh, I sure wish you were coming with us."

"Me, too. Take care of yourself, you big lug."

"Yeah." He wanted to say more. Gertie had let go of his arm and started for the recreation room. "Oh, Dink. Maybe you could call Gert once in a while when I'm gone. She's gonna be awful lonesome."

"Sure, Sam, don't you worry." Lonesomeness, I felt pretty sure, was not going to be one of Gertie's problems.

Other shipmates were arriving now and each had some clever witticism for me. "Keep a keen lookout there, Dink old by. Don't want this craft to flounder on the rocks tonight." Clever stuff like that. God how I hated the whole stupid lot!

The officers, of course, didn't come in through my door, but in the front door and straight to the wardroom where they had their own little party before coming out to join in the dancing. So it was quite a while before I saw Patricia.

One of Lightson's bumboys had opened up the bar in the canteen. None of your coke and soft drinks this night. Real hard stuff and beer, the profits from which would all go to that bastard Lightson.

The orchestra hired for the night began to play and everybody began to dance up a storm. I've noticed that you never really know a guy until you see him dance. Some of those sailors, whom I'd known for six weeks as rather stolid types, became something entirely different when they began to jitter-bug. Of all the dances that I've seen come and go, from the Charleston of the twenties to the flea hop and the bunny hug and twist and all the rest, to me the jitterbug best represents the joy and abandon that dancing should be. Man, how they did whirl and jump and pitch each other around.

Of course there were the usual fox trots and two steps and waltzes and a congo line, and somebody even tried to introduce the Lambeth walk. It was very big just then, as it had come from dear old England which was suffering such hell with the bombings.

After about the second or third dance, the officers and their ladies began coming out of the wardroom, and there, sure enough, with that lout Hotshot was Patricia. I couldn't help it. As soon as I saw her my gut turned to water and I got a heavy feeling in my chest. She came out of the wardroom hand in hand with Hotshot, swinging his hand and laughing. When she saw me she excused herself and came floating over to the quarterdeck.

"You really are on duty," she said.

"That's what I told you."

"But why?"

"Somebody's got to do it. Mine not to reason why, mine but to do and die."

"Oh!" Her expression changed then from one of saucy gaiety to compassion, and that got my gut even worse. "I'm so sorry."

"It's nothing. Go ahead and have a good time."

Whatever she might have said was cut off by Hotshot who came up and took her arm. "Keep a close lookout there, Diespecker," he quipped. "Don't let any enemy battleships sneak up Queen Street on us."

The only reply I could have made to that would have got me court martialed and so I let it go. It was time for one stroke of the bell to denote eight-thirty and I executed that manoeuvre.

Things, as they say, progressed. The music got louder, the dancing wilder, the laughter sillier and I madder. I simply couldn't take it any more; something was sure to bust. Mike did his best for me. Came over with a conspiratorial grin on his ugly puss, fished a bottle of coke out from under his jersey and smuggled it to me. "Try that. Make hair grow on your chest."

I tried it and found it well spiked with rum. I'm sure Mike's intentions were good, but a drink of rum just then was like throwing gasoline on an already raging fire.

"Seen Sam?" he asked.

"Yeah. He came in with Gert quite a while ago."

"That broad! Should see her dancing with Shiek LaRonge. Good thing they've got clothes on."

Pierre LaRonge was the woman killer of the ship's company. Tall and dark and greasy. When he first came he had long, dark sideburns down to his chin, but of course Lightson soon made him get rid of those. But even with the regulation haircut he managed the Rudolph Valentino look. Evidently he was irresistible to a lot of women and had already been to sick bay for interesting treatments.

But I couldn't worry about Sam just then. I was too mad myself. What was I going to do when they all marched gaily out the big front door and down Regal, behind the band playing "Colonel Bogey"?

And as that time approached, the madder I got. At ten forty-five the dancing stopped and the ship's company was mustered on the main deck. All guys I knew. I could see them from my post and a motley-looking group they made, grinning and weaving and talking. The C.O. came out, also grinning and weaving slightly, and made a little speech about what great fellows they were, and brave, and how they were going forward to uphold democracy and truth and honour and how they must never forget that they were navy and guardians of the proud traditions of Nelson. Then somebody, probably Harry Binns, shouted "Three Cheers for the Captain!" and they all cheered their fool heads off. Altogether a most disgusting scene.

There was one real tragedy. As they stood there grinning and weaving and as the C.O. was reaching the climax of his stirring address, there was a loud crash made by the falling of a bottle of rye on the concrete deck. A groan of woe rose from the entire ship's company. Most of the guys had mickeys on their persons so that they could continue their celebrations on the train, and the precious bottle had accidently slipped from under the jersey where it was being clutched.

Promptly at 2300 hours the right turn order was given and the men marched out the door. Mike and Sam both looked my way and gave a little wave as they went from my sight. I hated to see them go. Then for the first time I realized where they were going and what they were going to do. All the fun and partying aside, they were marching off to fight the foe, and there was a good chance I'd never see them again.

I could hear the band strike up and out on the street the sound of marching feet died away and I was alone. All alone. The officers that hadn't marched with the men had gone back into the wardroom, and the big, hollow garage was absolutely empty.

And I made up my mind that I wouldn't stay there alone. I'd had it with the navy, given them six weeks of earnest service and they had scorned me. Well, to hell with them. I'd go over the hill. Go to another town, change my name and join the army. That service asked few questions; if you were breathing they'd take you. If I'd waited until I went off duty at midnight I'd have had the whole weekend before being missed. Leaving my post was a more serious offence than straight desertion. But I was too mad to give consideration to that. I had to get out of there or bust.

So I started running out the door, and ran smack into a sailor coming in. He was about medium height, squarely built and wore the uniform of a chief petty officer. But it was his face that got me, wrinkled and windburned and ugly, much like the ugly face of Abraham Lincoln.

"Permission to come aboard?" he said in a deep voice, ignoring our collision, although he must have known that I was deserting my post.

94

Nobody had ever asked me for such permission before, but I answered, "Permission granted."

He stopped in front of me and looked me over carefully with big dark eyes.

"Place seems pretty well deserted."

"The draft has just marched off to catch the train east."

"I get it. They've just had their embarkation party."

"Yep. That's what they had."

"But you didn't go."

"Nope."

"Why not?"

I didn't answer and he changed his tack. "I'm Chief Petty Officer Muldoon, just off the corvette *Calgary*. First leave in six months. Thought maybe I might find somebody here to shoot the breeze with."

"Nobody here but some officers in the wardroom."

He made a face. "When are you off duty?"

I looked at my watch. "Fifteen minutes."

"Good. Maybe you'd do me the pleasure of having a drink with me. I know a good bootlegger on Pine Street. I'm sure he's still there. What about it?"

"Yeah, I'd like that. Hey, did you say that you've actually been to sea?"

"Hell yes. Been sunk twice. Damned lucky, actually. Almost got picked up by a German sub, but a flying boat landed and got us first. Thank God for that flying boat! Without it I'd be enjoying Herr Schicklgruber's hospitality for the rest of this affair."

"Gosh!" Here it was. The real thing. All the bullshit and regimentation and phoniness aside, this was what it was all about. Going to sea in a corvette on escort duty, fighting German subs, getting sunk. Wow!

As soon as I was off duty, Muldoon hailed a taxi and we went to the house on Pine Street. It was a big old frame house painted white, with a big veranda in front. When we rang the bell, a muffled female voice from inside said, "Who is it?"

"Open up, Marg, it's Muldoon!"

"Muldoon!" It was a shriek of pleasure. The door opened

wide – strictly against bootlegger's regulations – and a female figure came hurtling out into the ample arms of Muldoon. She covered his face with kisses; he carried her into the house and I followed, closing the door behind me.

We went into the big old livingroom and sank into big old stuffed chairs and chesterfield. The great thing about bootleggers is this business of not having to sit on hard chairs at little hard tables and quaff your beer in a hurry, with waiters looking sideways at you each time they pass to see if you are ready for another one.

Marg brought us beer in big glasses and Muldoon patted her tight little backside. "I'll check with you later, sweetheart. Right now I want to talk with this young feller. He needs talking to."

Marg sat down and listened, impatiently.

"So you were about to go over the hill, eh?" Muldoon said, sipping his beer.

It took me completely by surprise. "What? No."

"No use denying it. What the hell else were you doing flying out the door when I came aboard?"

"Well, I guess I had something like that in mind."

"Why'd you miss the draft?"

So I told him all about Lightson. Maybe it was because he'd taken off his jacket with the C.P.O. insignia on it and looked just like a friend.

He listened carefully, grunting now and then and rubbing his chin. When I'd finished, he said quietly, "Yeah, I understand. Coves like Lightson are hard to take. But you've got to take them. You'll get out of that dump some day and then you'll forget all about him."

"I don't know. The navy seems so . . . so . . . phony somehow."

"Seems that, but it ain't. Funny thing is that all the guff the C.O. throws at you about navy tradition and such is true. It's a great service. Doing an important job, too."

"How did you get into it?"

"Oh, I'd been in the reserves for years. Took a couple of cruises in peacetime and got this rating. Then when the war started I shipped to England right away and joined the Royal Navy. When we got some ships of our own I transferred back. I've known Lightson from away back. He's not such a bad guy in many ways. Knows his stuff. But he's vindictive."

"Nothing I do pleases him."

"I know. Some C.P.O.s are like that. They have favourites and they've got to have somebody to pick on. Like some teachers. Human nature."

The beer and Muldoon's calmness were working wonders with me. The world was beginning to look less black.

"Trouble with the setup at *Porpoise*," Muldoon went on, "is that Lightson has too much power. A good captain who knows the navy wouldn't let him take over so completely."

"Well, we're getting a new captain, Monday."

"Maybe he'll straighten out the place. Come on, lad, drink up. You're away behind."

So we drank and talked until I couldn't talk any more, and then Muldoon put me in a taxi and sent me home.

Maybe the new C.O. would make things better.

10

Naturally and Smartly

I joined the navy to see the world. And what did I see? I saw a garage.

Those words kept running through my head as I began my second hitch aboard HMCS *Porpoise*. Here I was, stuck, for what seemed to me an interminable additional six weeks. It was tough enough, Lord knows, going down to that crummy barracks every day and going through the same old stuff all over again, but worst of all was the attitude of friends and neighbours, or what I considered to be their attitude.

I found myself feeling like and, to some extent, acting like a draft dodger. Most of my classmates in the army, air force, or navy had by now been shipped out, and I got so I didn't feel too much like walking down the street in my naval uniform. Even my family was confused. Doug, who since my enlistment had become an expert on all things naval, came home from school one day with a bloody lip.

"Jimmy Peters," he explained when Ma insisted on an explanation, "that creep, just because his brother's overseas thinks he's something. But he's got no right to call Dink a zombie."

"Whatever in the world is that?" Ma asked, and well she might.

I should explain to anyone too young to remember, that this was a time when the words "draft dodger" and "zombie" were being kicked around pretty freely. Zombies were the men who joined the army for limited service in Canada and resisted all the pressures applied by the army brass to make them "go active." It was all part of Mackenzie King's double talk: "Conscription if necessary, but not necessarily conscription." A sort of voluntary conscription, a game of cat and mouse. Army officers trying to persuade, coerce, shame, and bully zombies into enlisting for overseas service and the zombies trying to resist.

One of my ex-classmates, who like me had been subjected to anti-war propaganda all through high school and who had sincere scruples about shooting people or ramming bayonets through their guts, had joined the reserves. "You've no idea, Dink," he told me, "the tricks they use to make us go active. Mother's boys, they call us, and give us all the dirty jobs around camp. I've scrubbed out so many latrines I stink like one. I've been called a coward in so many different ways that I'm beginning to feel like one. But they aren't going to get me."

But they did get him, finally, as they got most of them, and he was killed along with hundreds of others in the shallow waters off Normandy before he even got ashore on D-Day.

Actually that attitude had permeated HMCS *Porpoise* as well. C.P.O. Lightson seemed convinced that some of the new recruits had joined the navy merely to evade the draft. He'd stand in front of a group of fresh-faced kids, his lean face suffused with scorn, voice dripping with that special brand of sarcasm reserved for C.P.O.s. "If yu've jyned the naivy because you think it's a soft berth, you're jolly well soon going to learn differently. The Raiyl Canaidian Naivy is no plaice for draft dodgers or zombies." Why did I think he cast a sideways glance in my direction when he said that?

"You're becoming paranoid, Dink," Smiley warned me at Stand Easy. "You mustn't let it get to you."

Just then the new C.O. passed us. I sprang to attention and whipped up my best naval salute. He paused and returned the salute and seemed about to say something, but hurried on. He was a tall man, about six foot three, I judged, with a profile and a build something like that of Tyrone Power.

"Now there's a handsome bloke," I said when he was out of earshot. "What's he like?"

Smiley screwed his ugly puss into a grimace of distaste. "Lieutenant Commander Austin B. Featherby? Straight out of HMS *Pinafore*."

"Huh?"

"All spit and polish. And phony as a three-dollar bill."

"What do you mean, phony?"

"Well, he's a broker from Montreal. Never been to sea a day in his life, but, man, is he pusser. All navy. Read everything there is to read about the navy and insists the officers observe customs that were obsolete when Nelson was a kid. Ever hear of Dogs of War?"

"No, but I've heard of the Hounds of the Baskervilles."

"Funnee, funnee. Dogs of War is something the captain pulls on one of the junior officers by shouting, 'Dogs of War on Sub-Lieutenant Smith,' and then everybody jumps on Smith and pull his pants off. A wardroom game. And that's not the worst."

"Shut up, Smiley," I interrupted.

Now it was his turn to look surprised. "Wha . . .?"

"I don't want to hear any more about our esteemed captain. Far as I'm concerned, he's a wonderful guy and I'm going to get in good with him."

"Dink! You? Brown-nosing?"

"Call it what you like. You are looking at the new Diespecker. I'm going to keep my nose so clean around here even Lightson will love me. Mr. Goody Two-shoes, that's me. I'll co-operate with everybody, be nice to everybody, salute officers when they're a block away. There'll be no more black marks on the record of Diespecker R.E.F. I tell you."

The bosun piped Fall In and I fell in as smartly as any sailor can fall, and Smiley went back to his galley.

I meant it, too. Diligence, co-operation, strict attention to duty would be my watchword from that moment on. I would make C.P.O. Lightson consider me the best damned naval rating he'd ever encountered, not only on the prairies but on the whole blasted booming main.

I volunteered for every duty going. I assisted the new entries with their bends and hitches, practised semafore and Morse code with them by the hour; I was never late, never adrift, always ready and eager with a ready answer and a helping hand.

So it was with some self-satisfaction and smugness that I reported to C.P.O. Lightson, at his request, in his little office beside the canteen. All my good behaviour was surely about to bear fruit.

"Well, Diespecker," he said when I stopped before his desk. "So you've done it again."

"What?" There was no doubt he was looking about as perturbed as I'd ever seen him.

"How long have you been in the navy?" he roared.

"Why, just over seven weeks."

"And you still haven't learned the simplest rules!"

"I haven't?"

"Such as naval salutes and marks of respect!"

Here I knew I was on safe ground. One of my duties had been teaching the new entries this very subject. I began quoting from the manual: "The naval salute is made by bringing up the right hand to the cap, naturally and smartly, but not hurriedly, with the thumb and fingers closed together, elbow in line with the shoulder, hand and forearm in line, with the palm of the hand turned to the left, but inclined slightly inwards.

"When passing an officer. . . ."

"I know that!" Lightson roared. "But what about this? 'There is no excuse for not seeing an officer or for not recognizing an officer in plain clothes, who, whether on account of his rank or the fact that he belongs to the same unit as the man, should be known to him.'" Lightson was leaning forward across his desk, glaring at me like a dog straining at the leash.

"Oh I know that. Naval officers are permitted to wear mufti - civilian clothes -"

"I know what mufti means, you fathead!"

"Yes, of course. Unlike army and air force, officers can wear civilian clothes when off duty and the ratings . . ."

"Well?"

"Are supposed to salute them. And I assure you that I always do."

"Oh you do, do you? Then why do you suppose the Captain called me into his office to inform me that last night he met you in the lobby of the Capitol Theatre and you walked right by him without a salute of any kind?"

"Oh no!"

"Oh yes. And do you know what the Captain said to me? He said that it was obvious that the men hadn't been properly instructed. So you see it's a black mark against not you, Deespecker, but me!"

"Gosh, I'm sorry, Chief. I was with a girl and –"

"Not properly instructed. Well, I'm going to see to it that you are properly instructed! You will take your Manual of Seamanship and you will memorize every word of pages seven, eight, nine, and ten. Every bloody word! Do you understand?"

So much for my campaign to make Lightson love me. Now I was in the bad books of the Captain as well.

But the worst was yet to come, when Smiley and I both got a weekend off and I decided to introduce him to the wonders and delights of the Wabagoon Exhibition.

Ah, the Wabagoon Exhibition, how can I describe it? In my mind it will always rank first among the great fairs of the world. The Canadian National Exhibition in Toronto, the World's Fair in Montreal? Pale imitations.

It was always held during the last week of August, which was simply known as Fair Week. And it was always the hottest week of the year. In fact persons from other parts of the land, experiencing the harshness of the prairie climate for the first time, were known to observe that we had only two seasons – Winter and Fair Week.

One of the best parts of the week was the very beginning, when a bunch of us kids would hike the two miles out to the Exhibition Grounds and watch the Johnny J. Jones railway train arrive, with the entire midway packed into its brightly painted and oddly shaped cars.

I can see it all still. The track of the CNR ran right along beside the fair grounds and in the middle of the night, always the middle of the night, the cars would be unloaded while we kids stood by in awe and wonderment at the spectacle.

Torches ablaze to illuminate the scene, roustabouts shouting, tractors roaring and, most thrilling sight of all, the big grey elephants pushing with their foreheads and, gently as a woman moving a pram, slowly manoeuvring the big wagons off the flatcars, down the ramps to the ground. And on those wagons the cages with lions and tigers and monkeys and other wonders from afar. And sometimes we'd catch a glimpse of a beautiful woman in a gaudy costume, or a midget from the midget show or the thin man, or the fat lady waddling along with her child holding her hand. An ordinary child, imagine that? To think that such a glamorous person would have an ordinary child.

Once, I remember, there was great consternation and shouting and swearing and screaming when a crate was accidentally dropped and the giant python got loose. Thirty feet long, it was whispered among the onlookers, and capable of swallowing a full-grown man whole with one gulp. But they found the creature asleep under one of the wagons and peace was restored. It was something we talked about for months and, come to think of it, still talk about.

Then we'd troup into the grounds and watch the roustabouts setting up the tents and the rides and the games of chance, getting ready for the Monday morning opening, which was always Kids' Day.

Kids' Day! Everything was a nickel. For a dollar, saved up over the months, you could get in every show and on every ride in the grounds. We'd arrive early and leave late. I always tried to save a nickel for the streetcar ride home, but never managed it, succumbing always to the delicious corn on the cob skewered on a stick and bathed in a can of melted butter.

We saw everything. The motorcycle show where men in black leather leggings and helmets rode their bikes around the inside of a big bowl, gaining momentum until centrifugal force held them out straight from the wall, just a half foot below our heads where we were standing on a platform gazing down into the bowl. And the freak show where "that pretty little half boy" with nothing below his chest walked about on his hands and painted signs for the other shows and laughed and talked just like anyone. And the living skeleton, made that way, he said, by smoking cigarettes. And the attractive midgets in their tiny livingrooms dancing and singing for our entertainment.

Then in the afternoon we'd sneak into the grandstand to watch the horse races. An entire week of horse racing. And this followed by the greatest grandstand show that ever was, featuring the Coldstream Guards Band from England or, one year, a band from far-off Australia. Then the trapeze acts and the dancing girls, and one year an Australian with boomerangs and bullwhips. He could rake a cigarette out of the mouth of a pretty girl standing fifty feet away. And then the grand finale, the fireworks, with prairie heroes outlined in blazing lights and sky rockets bursting in the air. And then the long, long trudge home in the middle of the night, so tired we scarcely could put one foot ahead of the other.

I explained all these wonders to Smiley and he yawned and said that since there was nothing else to do we might as well give it a whirl.

We arrived at the fairgrounds shortly after noon, with a mickey of rye whiskey to protect against snake bite or frost bite or whatever. (Oh for the good old days of youth when we could get as high as kites on a few swallows of booze.) And in an amazingly short time we were staggering from ride to ride, happy as kids and completely oblivious of the fact that we were representatives of the King's Navee.

Ah, those rides. Up and down and around about they whirled us, jerking us this way, pitching us that, sometimes up-side down, sometimes high enough to see strawstacks in the fields five miles away.

Underneath the immense grandstand (everything about the Wabagoon Exhibition was immense) was a long enclosure where at open booths some of the more cultural activities of the city were displayed. And there, wonder of wonders, sitting on a stool attending a counter in front of an exhibit of paintings by local artists, was the light of my life, the subject of my dreams, the partner of my fantasies, none other than the beautiful, glamorous, gorgeous Patricia!

All my shyness completely diluted by alcohol, I swaggered up to the booth and leaning boozily over the counter shouted, "Well, look who's here! Patricia the fair, Patricia the lovable, Patricia the lily maid of. . . ."

"Robin!" she interrupted. "Stop it!"

"Robin? Robin, is it?" Smiley hooted. "Little Robin Redbreast sat upon a tree."

"Enough!" I roared. "Patricia, you must come with us and join our revels. We'll take you to paradise!" I began to sing a currently popular song featuring those very lines and executed a cute little dance on the concrete in front of the booth. Several art lovers paused to observe this display and poor Patricia burned red to the roots of her lovely hair.

"Robin, please, for goodness sake!"

"Will you come?"

"Certainly not! Now please go away. Can't you see you are – "

I felt a tug at my arm and Smiley's booze breath in my ear. "The shore patrol!"

Sure enough, a pair of those burly types were just entering the glass doors at the end of the enclosure.

"Who cares about the little ole shore patrol," I began, but Smiley grabbed my arm and dragged me into the crowd, luckily before the shore patrol burlies could see us. He hauled me along and through a door marked Men, into a room with a long line of basins, urinals and booths. We entered one of the booths, latched the door and proceeded to fortify ourselves. By this time the raw whiskey slid down our throats smooth as water, and we each took a couple of good belts.

"Come on," I shouted. "Let's ride the airplanes and shoot down Germans!"

This was in reference to a wonderful ride that looked like a giant maypole, with twelve or so arms sticking out from the top of a fifty-foot perpendicular steel post. Attached to the end of each arm by twenty-foot chains was a small model of an aircraft, complete with short wings, a tail and a seating capacity for two. As the central pole turned faster and faster, driven by a small gas engine, the planes swooped and zoomed at a marvellous speed.

After waiting in line for fifteen minutes and making asses of ourselves with our witty comments, Smiley and I finally managed to get into one of our planes, buckled our seat belts, adjusted our imaginary machine guns and got ready to blast German Messerschmidts from the sky. And we did, too, laughing and shouting as the foul ME 109's bit the dust before us. Then as we began to slow down for a landing, I began to get an extemely funny feeling in my gut, and at the same time noticed below among the crowd a most unsavoury sight. None other than our esteemed C.O. and with him none other than the light of my life, Patricia.

Oh the perfidity of it. The foulness, the rottenness of it all! My darling and that wolf! For already, although he had been with us only a short time, our captain had gained a considerable reputation as a ladies' man. In the wardroom, Smiley had informed me, he usually turned up with a different beauty every evening. (There were a goodly number of lonely unattached women about, of course, whose husbands or boyfriends were otherwise employed in far away places, and a dashing young naval officer could just about have his pick.) Like a hog sniffing out truffles, he had found his way to the gorgeous Patricia.

Back on the ground, our gaits even more unsteady because of the dizzying effect of the whirls we'd taken, I told Smiley what I'd seen and insisted that we keep the pair of them in sight.

"What the hell for?" Smiley wanted to know.

"Protection, that's what for. That poor innocent girl and that suave, debonair man of the world. She'll be like putty in his hands." (Under the influence I tend to lean heavily towards the more obvious clichés.)

"You're crazy. That's what you are, Dink, crazy as a hoot

owl. Supposing you're right, what could possibly happen to her in a crowd like this?"

"They could get out of the crowd. Come on!" I grabbed his arm and dragged him towards the spot where I thought I saw them.

But of course they weren't there. I kept going, dragging Smiley and bumping into people right and left as I attempted to weave my way through the happy throng. Then I spotted them up ahead. They were standing together among a small group of people in front of a stand on which stood a swarthy character with black hair down to his shoulders and dressed as an Indian. He was holding a lethargic rattlesnake in both hands and explaining how the venom from the creature could cure anything from backache to ingrown toenail.

"Rattlesnake oil, my friends, an ancient remedy of the Hopi Indians who have dwelled for centuries in the Painted Desert of the U.S. The venom of the snake mixed with the fat of the carcass, boiled for just the right length of time and mixed with certain herbs, the secret of which has never been divulged, and you have a remedy that is beyond the dreams of modern medicine. Observe."

He poured some of the stuff from a bottle onto a thick piece of leather and showed how it penetrated to the other side in a matter of seconds. "Will your liniment, prescribed by your learned doctors, match that? Imagine if it can go through that thick leather how it will penetrate your skin and get to the aching muscles beneath. Only a dollar, my friends, for a bottle of this -"

"Hey, that looks pretty good, Dink," Smiley said. "Lend me a dollar."

But from the corner of my eye I noticed that our quarry was leaving the group and strolling on through the crowd, laughing and - horrors - holding hands.

"Come on!" I shouted. "Mustn't lose 'em."

"What the hell is wrong with you?"

"Gotta protect." I dragged him away at a run.

"You know something funny?" Smiley panted as he tried to keep up. "The Old Man is improperly dressed."

"Mufti. It's permitted. Read it in the manual."

"Sure, civilian dress is permitted, but he's got the khaki trousers of his summer uniform on. Look like just ordinary trousers, but they ain't. Strictly against regulations to use part of a uniform. It's the whole thing, including cap, or nothing."

What happened from that point on never was very clear in my mind. Most of it was reported to me by Smiley, who either remembered or made it up.

Anyway, I had spotted my quarry standing in front of the candy floss booth, both with big cones of the sticky stuff in their hands, laughing and joking about how they were going to eat it. A most disgusting sight. And me, boiling full steam ahead towards them with no more idea of what I'd do when I got there than a rowboat approaching a battleship.

What I did was to pull up short in front of the Captain, raise myself to my full five-feet-eleven-and-a-half and whip up a perfect naval salute.

My sudden arrival, my wild and frantic appearance, and most of all my salute took him completely by surprise. Involuntarily he began to raise his right hand to his forehead, realized in time that he'd fill his hair with goo if he did, attempted with dignity to shift it to his left hand, and smeared it on his shirt in the process. All of which gave me time to go into my spiel.

My head was brim full of the stuff I'd memorized from the manual and now it gushed from my mouth like water from a fireman's hose:

"Point Two. When an officer or rating is without his cap or helmet or is carrying anything which prevents him saluting with his right hand, if standing still he is to stand at attention and face an officer who passes; if walking, he is to turn his head and eyes smartly –"

But that's as far as I got. Smiley, who'd been listening in stunned disbelief to this, suddenly came to life, grabbed me by the arm and half-pulled, half-lifted me out of there.

"Shore patrol!" he hissed as we dissolved into the crowd, and from the corner of my eye I beheld our two friends, obviously attracted by my tirade, approaching the Captain and engaging him in earnest conversation.

It was explained to me afterwards, first by Smiley and then by Lightson, that even officers are not immune to being checked up by the shore patrol if they are improperly dressed.

"Oh, the Captain is going to love you from now on," Lightson added with a shake of his handsome head. "He really is!"

11

Deeper and Deeper

As can be imagined, my status aboard HMCS *Porpoise* didn't improve following my performance at the Exhibition. Now, not only was I considered to be the choice bungler of all time, but I was actually the C.O.'s rival for the favours of Patricia.

The only mitigating circumstance was the arrival of Schoolie.

Schoolmaster is a traditional rank in the Royal Navy and in the Royal Canadian Navy. His job is to bring the ratings up to a required standard in English and arithmetic, and to assist leading seamen and others who are bucking for promotion and who need upgrading in their education. The navy had the odd notion that ratings should be able to spell, write a decent sentence, know a little grammar, and be at home with fractions, decimals, averages, and other such old-fashioned stuff.

There were tests given regularly that all ratings had to pass if they hoped to be promoted. They were E.T.1 (Education Test One), the E.T.2 and the E.T.3.

And so it came to pass that the navy in its wisdom decided that each of the naval divisions across the country should have a schoolmaster or, as he was always called by ratings and officers alike, a schoolie. And since *Porpoise*, for all it had the definite appearance of an ancient garage, qualified as a *bona fide* naval division, we got one.

We had our first introduction to Sub-Lieutenant (Special Branch) Dydell through none other than my old nemesis Lightson. He sat us down at some tables that had been lined up in the recreation room, where a makeshift blackboard had been set up on a rickety tripod, and he informed us thus:

"Pay attention, men, from now on you are going to take school classes. Regular part of your training. God knows some of you can use it, judging from the way you talk. The officer in charge of the school is Sub-Lieutenant Dydell. Like the M.O. and the paymaster, he is what is known as Special Branch. Where the M.O. wears a white stripe above or between his braid, the schoolmaster wears light blue. Any questions?"

"Please, Chief, will he make us stand in the corner if we chew gum?" This was from an immense stoker who was noted for his humorous quips.

"Very funny. But let me tell you, the schoolmaster is a regular commissioned officer, same as the executive officer or the captain and the rest, and is to be treated by ratings in the same way. Understand? You salute him. You call him sir and you bloody well do what he tells you. He can put you on charge the same as any other officer. So you're not going to get away with anything with him."

The ship's company looked decidedly sad and not a little apprehensive. Educationally, we ran the gamut of practically none to university graduates. Ordinary Seaman Prowle had a Ph.D. in philosophy. He told a story about the recruiting officer who, after perusing his list of degrees from four universities, looked up and remarked impatiently, "Yeah, but it doesn't say here whether or not you've got your senior matric."

I remember Diddle (it didn't take long for the ratings to pin that handle on him) as well as I do any officer I encountered in the R.C.N.V.R. He was a short man and thin, with an exceptionally small head so that his officer's cap always appeared to be about to slide down over his eyes. He was a quiet man with absolutely no swagger, which gave the impression of weakness, prompting some, who remembered their childhood schoolteachers with hatred, to try some of their sneaky tricks on him.

These consisted of the standard gimmicks: loud belches, imitation farts made by placing the mouth against the wrist and forcing air through, witty asides, dropping books on the floor and the like. Diddle simply ignored them all. He'd been a schoolteacher for more than ten years and had encountered and handled just about every nasty type. The thing was that nobody quite dared to go much further. After all Diddle wasn't a teacher; he was a naval officer and officers have teeth. Besides, there's no fun teasing somebody who doesn't get mad.

So we got down to work at spelling, composition, arithmetic, and grammar. I suppose the two things that have accounted for more downright misery and frustration in grade school (I understand they don't teach them much any more) are common fractions and the formal rules of English grammar.

Common fractions? Okay, here's one for you. What is one-quarter divided by one-eighth? This was one of Diddle's favourites, used on new recruits with from Grade Four to university education, just to show them they weren't as smart as they thought they were. Get it? If you said anything but two you need a dose of Diddleism.

The image of grown men chewing on stubs of pencils trying to figure out whether to use "lain" or "laid" will always remain with me, although I could never figure out how it helped the war effort.

Diddle became a tired old man trying to explain the intricacies of the two verbs. His explanations went something like this:

"Lie is always an intransitive verb, having no object. For instance, 'I lie down on the couch.' Lay, on the other hand, is always transitive, having an object, 'I lay the book on the desk.' Always remember that simple rule."

Simple! Hell, he lost most of us when he used the words "transitive" and "intransitive." And what the hell was an "object"?

"Now," Diddle would fight manfully on, "the confusion is

confounded by the fact that the past tense of 'lie' is 'lay' and so here 'lay' becomes an intransitive verb, as in 'I lay down yesterday,' and the past participle of 'lie' is 'lain.' Understand?"

We would all nod stupidly, most of us having been distracted by the word 'lay,' which we knew all right, as in 'She was a good lay.' Musing on this delightful thought we'd tend to miss Diddle's further explanation.

"Now we come to the past tense of the transitive verb 'lay,' which is 'laid,' as in 'I laid the book on the table,' or 'I have laid the book on the table,' the past participle being the same as the past tense."

And so it went. Big fat blue-bottles droned about the hot, smelly room and we tried to catch them with our hands as they landed. Some of us dozed off, emitting soft, bubbly snores that competed with the sound of the blue-bottles; other had pleasant fantasies of girls in every port, especially those with swaying hips covered with grass skirts, all far removed from the grim realities of the North Atlantic.

The arithmetic problems, which came from a green, hard-covered text long used by the Royal Navy, were somewhat more practical if no less obtuse. "If a ship steams at a speed of ten knots for fifteen minutes, slows to four knots for twenty-five minutes, stops completely half an hour and then steams at a speed of eight knots for two hours, what is its average speed?"

Try that on your harmonica.

Most of us never mastered it, although Diddle repeatedly told us that "the simple rule for finding average speed is to divide the total distance travelled by the total time."

Besides being a teacher, Diddle, as the only more-or-less permanent officer aboard, was also the recreation officer and sports officer. He taught us the R.C.N.V.R. song, which goes:

"Roll along, Wavy Navy, roll along,
Roll along, Wavy Navy, roll along,
When they ask us who we are
We're the R.C.N.V.R.,
Roll along, Wavy Navy, roll along."

Diddle would sit at the old upright piano and pound out the tune while the ship's company roared out the words. Some never got them straight and would invariably sing:

"When they ask us who we screw,
We reply, 'The whole damned crew,' "

Diddle also arranged shows in which all members of the ship's company were urged to participate. Naval policy encouraged such shows for not only did they relieve the monumental boredom of service life but they provided an opportunity for officers and ratings to get drunk together and break down the barriers of rank. This rapport was especially important to the navy. In the cramped living and working quarters aboard a corvette being pitched about by twenty-foot seas of the North Atlantic, it was too easy for unpopular officers to disappear mysteriously over the side.

The first show that Diddle organized, directed, and acted in should have been a great success, but due to that horrible thing known as "a combination of circumstances" it was a complete disaster.

Schoolie was full of ideas. He'd been a great fan of The Dumbells, the hottest Canadian show of the late twenties and early thirties, and he had used most of their skits at scout camps. Besides, in common with many schoolteachers, he was an inveterate ham.

Diddle's favourite skit was the old music-hall turn known as "the hat trick," for which three characters were required. He asked Smiley and me to be his accomplices. Smiley was a natural choice for, along with his swagger, he'd had some experience on the stage. I don't know why he picked me for the third character, but I'm pretty sure that for the rest of his life he wished he hadn't.

The skit begins, as I'm sure anyone over the age of fifty will know, with two friends meeting centre stage. One of them, Schoolie, is terribly angry and when the other, Smiley, enquires of the reason Schoolie begins a tirade that goes like this:

"You want to know why I'm upset? I'll tell you. I'm not upset, I'm furious, I'm flaming mad!"

"Why is that?" Smiley asks.

"Why? I'll tell you why. About an hour ago I'm walking down this very street with my girl Susie on my arm. You know Susie?"

"A very pretty girl."

"And a real lady, don't forget that. Well, we meet Stoker Waldo, and when we come up to him I greet him in a friendly manner and I tip my cap."

"Why?"

"Because, stupid, don't you know anything about manners? That's what a gentleman always does when he's walking with a lady and meets a friend."

"He does?"

"Absolutely, and if the friend is a gentleman he will tip his cap too, in respect to the lady, you understand."

"I guess so."

"But not Waldo. He just grunts and keeps right on walking. Imagine. So you know what I do?"

"What?"

"Excusing myself from the lady, I go back and I stop Waldo and I say, 'Didn't you see that I'm walking with a lady?' and he says, 'Yeah, a dish.' And I say, 'Didn't you see me tip my cap out of respect for that lady?' and he says, 'Yeah,' and I say, 'Then why didn't you tip your cap?' and he says, 'I forgot,' and I says, 'Oh, you forgot, did you? I'll teach you to forget!' and I grab his cap off his head like this (taking Smiley's cap off his head) and I put in on the ground like this and I jump up and down on it like this (jumping on cap). Goodbye." He stomps off the stage, leaving stupid Smiley staring after him in dismay.

So, while Smiley is picking up his ruined cap, I come in from the other side of the stage. Smiley sees me and, by facial expression, indicates that he's going to play the same trick on me.

All goes well until the very end when I interrupt Smiley's

spiel and say, "That's a fine-looking cap you're wearing," take the cap off Smiley's head to inspect it more closely and cleverly exchange it for my own. Whereupon Smiley snatches his own cap off my head and, much to the glee of the audience, grinds it into the dirt.

We found a couple of old caps that belonged to nobody and with a generous application of white shoe polish made them look shiny new.

Fine. Schoolie rehearsed us until we had our parts down pat. Smiley caught on immediately and was very good. Luckily, since I had no stage experience whatsoever, I had practically nothing to say. I just had to stand there and mug at the audience and at the right moment exchange my cap for Smiley's. Simplicity itself. Except that during my stint aboard *Porpoise* nothing was simple.

Came the night of the show. The recreation room filled with rows of folding chairs borrowed from the Legion Hall and these were soon packed with officers and ratings and their girlfriends. Most of the officers had foregathered in the wardroom before the show and were feeling no pain. Most of the ratings had bought mickeys of rye which they worked on throughout the show. It was, to say the least, a joyous crowd.

Determined to beat the Captain's time, I had invited Patricia long before the evening, and she, somewhat reluctantly, agreed to come with me. But on the night of the show the Old Man out-manoeuvred me again by gallantly inviting both of us to sit with him at his place of eminence in the front row. Patricia beamed with delight, and I, of course, had to go along.

A stage of sorts had been constructed by pushing four platforms together, with a wire strung across for a curtain. The show was marvellous, as a show can only be when cast and audience are stewed to the gills. The chorus line of burly stokers wearing frilly skirts and tin-cup brassiers along with their issue clodhoppers were a riot. A sick-bay tiffy recited "The Cremation of Sam McGee," two subbies did a tap dance, and the new recruiting officer, displaying a fine Irish tenor voice, left nary a dry eye in the house with his rendition of "Going Home."

Came the time for our skit.

For the life of me, even now after all these years, I can't figure out why things happened the way they did. It was a simple enough exercise and I knew exactly what I had to do. But for one thing I'd been nipping away pretty steadily at the rye and my head was full of fuzz. Add to that the fact that the Old Man, also well along, was making a definite play for Patricia and she was reacting in a decidedly coltish manner. Besides, being that close to her always made me a blithering fool. Add to this my natural funk at getting on the stage at all and you have it.

Anyway, when Smiley went backstage to join Diddle who, of course, was already there, I remained in my seat and, like a dumb nut, sat and watched the first part of the skit. So when Diddle jumped on Smiley's cap I roared with laughter along with the rest. Then Schoolie peeked out from behind the curtain and motioned frantically for me to get with it.

At that point Patricia, who knew the skit, said, "It'll be much funnier this way," and grabbed the Old Man's cap from his knee and stuck it on my head, and he, who also knew the skit, let her. This all happened in a few seconds with the crowd roaring with laughter at Smiley inspecting his ruined cap.

So I got around the end of the curtain and staggered on the stage at just the right moment. Smiley spotted me and his face lit up with glee as he mugged to the audience that he'd play the same trick on me. And when that audience saw whose cap I was wearing and anticipated what was about to happen to it, their joy and enthusiasm knew no bounds.

Smiley approached me with a big stupid grin on his face and attempted to repeat Schoolie's spiel. Of course he got it all mixed up and the more laughs he got from the drunken ratings the more he hammed. As for me, I again confused my role between spectator and actor and became so intrigued by his performance that I forgot all about why I was up there, with the result that I completely forgot to interrupt him at the crucial moment and exchange caps as I was supposed to do. Maybe Smiley in his enthusiasm didn't notice the oversight, or maybe the idea of leaping on the Old Man's cap was too much for him. At any rate, that's exactly what he did, again and again, completely demolishing it.

Whatever else, it was an artistic success. The roar of laughter and hooting and whistling that issued forth from over a hundred well-oiled throats could have been heard at City Hall. There was no doubt that my neglect had greatly improved the skit.

There was also no doubt that it most definitely didn't improve my standing with the Old Man. Whatever my position had been on his shit list, this surely moved me to the top.

Whether or not it had anything to do with what happened in the boxing tournament, which followed shortly afterwards, I'll never know.

12

To Hit
Without Getting Hit

The Monday after our show, instead of being dismissed after opening exercises we were left standing at attention while Lightson reported to the Old Man. A little shudder of apprehension ran through the ranks, for we knew that when the commanding officer spoke to us it could only mean trouble.

We were right.

He stood there looking very natty in his freshly pressed blues and his new cap, and informed us that on our behalf he had issued a challenge to the commanding officer of Number Ten Air Training School of the RCAF to a boxing card.

He explained that not only would it be good for us, but since it would be held in the hockey arena it would provide entertainment for the civilian population. He said that match-ups would be made in all weight categories, and gave us a little pep talk on the importance of boxing in the armed services.

"Boxing," he said, "is an education. You learn self-control, to give and to take, to punish and be punished, smiling all the time."

To say that the Old Man liked boxing is like saying squirrels are mildly interested in nuts. He was crazy about boxing.

He loved boxing. To him it was the manly art, the true test, the ultimate contest, the measure of a man. The idea of punishing and being punished gave him a real high – just so long as somebody else was doing the punishing and getting punished. He would take care of the smiling.

I don't know where he got the quote. Probably from some book. He was a great one for second-hand quotes about manliness and true tests. Anyway, now that the softball season was over and we had won the inter-service championship, boxing was the thing that would absorb the interests of the athletically inclined ratings of HMCS *Porpoise*.

Group Captain Gorson, a craggy-faced First World War flier who was commanding officer of Number Ten Initial Training School of the RCAF, was also a raving, slavering boxing nut. So, a good healthy rivalry developed between the two men. I always thought that the best way for them to have settled it would have been to put on the gloves themselves and, like Sohrab and Rustum, have at each other to the death. But then I had nothing to do with the arrangements, and I suspect the idea of such a one-on-one contest never entered the minds of these two raw-meat tigers.

It so happened that at the time *Porpoise* had a real boxer. His name was Howard Wilbur Transvil, but he was always called Turk. About my size, but considerably better built, Turk was a mild-mannered, pleasant fellow of about twenty-five. A bricklayer by trade, he'd had a number of professional fights and had gained for himself the title of Middleweight Champion of Western Canada. This last fact we were instructed to keep from the air force.

I liked Turk and he liked me. The first time I boxed with him I learned the difference between a professional and an amateur. His punches were solid, even when he was holding back, as he did with me, and they were so quick that I never saw them coming. He taught me how to put my body behind my own punches so as to make them more solid. He also taught me how to handle the small bag and hit the heavy bag without injury to my wrists and how to skip rope.

When the Old Man saw Turk boxing, his enthusiasm for the sport increased tremendously. He even put on the gloves with Turk himself. Watching this encounter, I remember how I wished it were me in there against the Old Man and that I were as solid a hitter as Turk.

The best man the air force had at the Initial Training Base was also a middleweight. His name was Rostough and he'd been a plunging back for a professional football team. In the off-season he did quite a bit of boxing, and the word was that he'd knocked out all his opponents. Gorson was sure he could do the same to Transvil, and Featherby was just as sure that he couldn't.

Thus it came about that all our recreation time was taken up with training for the big boxing card. First came the weigh-ins, where every man who looked as though he could lift a boxing glove was weighed in the nude, to determine in just what weight class he fitted.

I weighed in at 162 pounds and was immediately instructed by the Old Man to get that weight down to less than 160 so that I could qualify as a middleweight. I didn't quite understand how I was to do this since, at that stage, I had little extra fat anywhere.

Then training for the final showdown between navy and air force began.

"Don't ever forget," the Old Man admonished us, "that the navy is not only the senior service, but also the superior service. You aren't just fighting for yourselves, you are fighting to uphold the reputation and honour of His Majesty's Navy." He failed to mention that we were also fighting so that he could win a one-hundred-dollar bet from Gorson.

The ten of us upon whose frail shoulders the reputation of His Majesty's Navy rested were, except for Turk, a motley group. We had no flyweight, but we did have a bantam, a skinny little guy named Rowels who was a Métis from Duck Lake. He had got into the navy as a cook, I suppose on the supposition that if he was strong enough to lift a soup ladle he could cook. Among the host of other flakey ideas that inhabited the Old Man's handsome dome was the one that any man with a drop of Indian blood in his veins was a natural killer. Actually, Rowels was a peaceful little guy who, at the tender age of seventeen, had already acquired his senior matric and was determined to become a doctor after the war. He didn't say much, but his words when they did come were carefully weighed and tended to be rather ponderous.

Like the rest of us, Rowels was over the 113-pound limit for bantams, but the Old Man was confident he could pare that down.

We also had a featherweight, a farm boy named Dornoski, who was very short and very wide. So far as I could ever gauge, he had no neck at all, just a big head sitting on a pair of Charles Atlas-like shoulders. He was immensely strong and could climb a rope with ease without using his feet at all. He'd just grab it and hand over hand himself to the top. I rather pitied anyone that the air force might match against him.

We had two lightweights, and in this class there was some controversy. The weight limit for the class, according to American rules, is 135 pounds, but by British rules it is an even ten stone, or 140 pounds. Naturally, the Old Man, who was British to the toenails, insisted on the 140-pound limit. Both of the tigers we had for the class, a stoker named Gluck and a writer named Barstow, might possibly get down to 140 pounds but could never be sufficiently pared to meet the lower weight.

There was, of course, a plethora of welterweights from which to choose. They had one thing in common, none of them knew the first thing about boxing. There was a sick bay tiffy named Arsenol, whose name, like mine, would make a fighter out of anyone; Ordinary Seaman Corbett, who at least had a good name for a boxer, but who moved like the famous Gentleman Jim as a plough horse moves like a racehorse. And then there was Ronce who, when picked for the slaughter, remarked, "Well, I might as well get killed in the ring as on some gawddamned ship."

We had two lightheavies. A big blond Swede from down south named Warse, who was surely one of the best hockey players ever to come out of the prairies, but whether he could box or not was another question. But whereas Warse was a natural athlete, the other lightheavy, a shy grain buyer of about thirty years of age, was anything but. I suspect he was picked because Lightson hated him almost as much as he hated me and, in his sadistic way, was looking forward to both of us getting our brains knocked out.

So there, as they say, is your boxing team. Let's hear it for them. Our training began at once. Diddle, who from his Boy Scout days believed in being prepared, somehow got boxing mixed up with marathon running. His idea of preparing us to meet the air force tigers was to get us out in our navy blue shorts and run the chuffs off us. We ran to the edge of town and then along dry, dusty roads straight out over the prairie, with the harvested wheat fields on either side, the bemused country folk staring at us as though we'd gone mad. Which we had.

Actually I became very fond of the road work. Because out there on the outskirts of the city on Queen Victoria Road there was a farm implement dealer named Brick - famous for Brick tractors - in whose office Patricia worked as a stenographer. And so I took to doing extra road work, which was readily agreed to since I knew all my bends and hitches, knots and splices and the rest of the stuff backwards. This extra road work consisted of running as far as Patricia and spending a half hour or so in her delightful company.

The only flaw in this arrangement was Patricia's eagerness to talk about Lieutenant Commander Featherby. "Don't you think he's the most distinguished-looking man?"

"Yeah. Distinguished. They tell me the wolf who met Red Riding Hood had the same air of distinction."

"What do you mean?"

"Well, I'm not giving away any secrets, since everybody knows it, when I say the Old Man will try to make anything in skirts."

"That's just gossip. His manners are perfect."

"Didn't your father ever warn you against guys like him?"

"Don't be silly. I think he's charming."

"Think what you like, but don't let him get you alone. Especially if he's got a snootful of those pink gins."

"Silly. He's asked me to go to a supper dance with him at the Colonial Hotel."

"Jees. You didn't accept?"

"Not exactly. But I may. I've never been to one of those dances. They say they're marvie. You're just jealous."

She was right, of course. Jealous as hell. But I think I was really concerned for her, too. Another time we talked about the boxing match for which I was supposed to be training.

"Why box anyway?" she pouted. "It's just silly, punching somebody in the head and getting punched back."

"And smiling," I added. "Don't forget the smiling."

"But why do it?"

"It's my duty. The Old Man says box, I box. We're in a war, you know. What do you want me to do, be a shirker?"

"Oh that's just silly."

She was right again, but a surprising number of things that are obviously silly and crazy and insane in peacetime seem absolutely logical in time of war. Like Patricia, I had a sneaking suspicion then of the absurdity of the whole operation, and in the light of what's happened since then, how right we were.

It became perfectly obvious that not one of the tigers we'd selected was making any progress whatsoever along the lines of becoming a boxer. Diddle had taught them how to stand with left foot and left hand extended towards the opponent, and had emphasized that they were to keep their feet in that position and not take a step forward or back, but rather to shuffle forwards and backwards. "Maintain balance at all times," he commanded, "ever ready to move without losing that balance and ready to strike the opponent with either hand."

Turk's instructions tended to be more direct. "For chrissake hit him! This isn't a game of pattycake, you know. You've got to put some weight behind those punches or you'll get killed!"

Diddle and the Old Man discouraged such talk. They

wanted our tigers to think of it as a game of pattycake, otherwise they knew damned well we'd all quit. I never in my life saw a group of men so gullible concerning something that was going to happen to them. The only thing I can compare it to, in the light of my vast experience, is an operation for piles. Everybody tells you, especially your doctor, that there is nothing to it. And you think there will be nothing to it and so you blissfully go to sleep on the operating table counting backwards, and then you wake up with a pain in your anus so excrutiating, so absolutely mind-boggling that if you'd known about you'd never have consented to the operation in a million years.

So it was with our tigers. I can see them now, blissfully trying to skip rope and stumbling over their own feet, pecking away at the punching bag, dancing about in the ring and making tentative little jabs at each other, with Diddle yelling, "That's it, chaps, you're getting it. That's right, counterpunch, counterpunch!" There wasn't one of them could punch his way through a piece of toilet paper.

At least that's what I thought.

And then events took a turn towards disaster. I first got wind of it two days before the fight card was to be staged, at one of our training sessions when the boxers were prancing around the deck making ineffectual jabs at nothing. Diddle, I noticed, had a look on his thin face that was decidedly grim. I'd never seen him looking like that before, and I was puzzled until he called me over and told me the reason, and then I was devastated.

"Oh, Diespecker," he began, "I've got something to tell you."

"My opponent has dropped dead from fear?"

"No. Nothing like that. I don't know how to tell you this, and I want you to know I had nothing to do with it."

"I've been scratched. Well, that's okay, sir."

"No. Stoker Transvil has been scratched."

"What? Why?"

"It's that wretched air force C.O. He heard about Transvil

125

being middleweight champion of western Canada and he says he's a professional."

"So?"

"Well, he won't go through with the tournament unless we find another middleweight to fight Rostough."

"But we haven't got another middleweight, except . . ." I had a horrible empty feeling in the region of my bowels. "No, you can't mean me!"

"That's what has been suggested."

"Me? Box with that guy? That's ridiculous, sir, crazy! Who ever got an idea like that?"

"Well, the scuttlebut around the ship here is that you knocked out a sub-lieutenant who was practically a professional boxer."

"No, no, we were just fooling around. It was a lucky punch and I didn't knock him out. Just knocked him down. He probably slipped."

"Whatever happened, it gave you a reputation."

"But, sir, this is awful. I can't. Besides, half the guys on the ship have bet on Transvil."

"They've bet on the main bout. I'm afraid the air force men they've bet with will insist on their honouring the bets."

"This gets crazier and crazier. Sir, you've got to . . ."

"I told you, it's not my idea. I'm sick about the whole thing. With Transvil in there we'd have had a good card."

"Then we'll have to call the whole thing off."

"We can't do that. Over five thousand tickets have been sold. All the publicity the newspaper and radio station have given us." He smiled weakly. "After all, it's only three rounds."

"A man can get killed in three rounds! Listen. Can the navy make me do this?"

"No, technically they can't. But the Captain and Lightson can put a lot of pressure on you."

"Don't I know it!"

"I can't promise you anything, of course, but if you do this it might make a difference. Besides, it would show Chief Petty Officer Lightson . . ."

"Show him what? What's he got to do with this?"

"Nothing. Except he said . . ."

"What?"

"Well, I guess he didn't really mean it."

"What did he say?"

"Oh, I forget his exact words. Something about your being too yellow to do it."

"He said that, eh?"

"I'm sure he didn't mean it."

"He meant it. I'll show that sonofabitch." It came out before I realized it. And that's how I became the navy representative in the main bout in the infamous boxing card at Wabagoon Arena in front of thousands.

13

Lambs to
the Slaughter

Wabagoon's biggest and, for all I know, only boxing card was held in the downtown arena where the senior and junior hockey games were played. It wasn't a big arena but not small either, with banks of seats along each side and a few at each end. A ring had been erected in the centre of what was normally the ice surface, and the space between it and the boards filled with folding chairs. These were the dollar seats. The regular arena seats, or rather benches, cost fifty cents.

The first shock to our boxers – other shocks would come later – was the number of people who came. Long before the first fight was to commence the place was jammed to the rafters.

"Holy Palooka!" was the comment of our lightweight Barstow. "We got to get up in front of all these people?"

The Old Man, resplendent in his best dress uniform, and his officers filled the seats along the west side of the ring, while the seats on the east side were occupied by Gorson and his bevy of brass. At the north end sat Diddle and the air force sports officer who, along with a neutral representative from the local YMCA, were to judge the bouts. A couple of sports writers from the local paper sat next to them, along with a cameraman to record the event for posterity.

The mayor of Wabagoon and sundry other VIPs were on the south side. All wore evening clothes and all the ladies wore long gowns. Most of these had been guests at a cocktail party in the *Porpoise* wardroom since about five in the afternoon and were, to say the least, in a festive mood. So, for that matter, were the rest of the members of this eager fight crowd. The ordinary seamen and the air force chaps had had their own little gatherings in the beer parlours and had placed their bets.

I can still see those fine ladies with their fancy hairdos and well made-up countenances, flushed with booze, peering expectantly and happily up into that ring. None of the females had ever seen a boxing match except perhaps a short shot in a news reel, and they had no idea what a fight was like. They would find out.

The fight announcer was some yahoot from the air force who stood in the middle of the ring and bleated "Ladeees and Gentulmen," in a poor imitation of Clem McCarthy, whom we used to hear on radio. "Tonight, in this ring, thirrreee rounds of boxing between the best of the navy and the best of the air force."

Wild cheering from the assembled throng, like unto that which I imagine greeted the lions and the Christians in the Roman Colosseum.

The bouts began with the smallest men, appetizers before the main feast, and that meant that Rowels was the first man in the ring for us. His opponent looked about twice as heavy as he but I may have been prejudiced; besides, I was watching the fight from the passageway that led to our dressing rooms under the west side seats.

As Rowels passed me in the passageway, wearing an old gabardine over his shoulders, I whispered, "Good luck!" but he didn't answer. His eyes were glazed and unseeing, like those of a calf going up the ramp behind the judas goat into the slaughterhouse. He reached the ring and climbed in and sat down on a stool in the corner where Steward Smiley and Sick Bay Tiffy Reagan were waiting for him. They pinched his shoulders and flabbed his muscles as they thought they were supposed to do. The referee announced the first bout, three rounds of three minutes each, and the fighters advanced to the centre of the ring.

At the bell Rowels went in there, as he'd been taught, with his left hand extended, shuffling along in a daze. He made a tentative little flick of a glove towards his opponent, whereupon his opponent hit him hard on the nose and sent him back on the seat of his pants on the floor. Blood spurted from his nose and splashed on some of the ladies at ringside. Two of them screamed and one fainted dead away after shrieking, "It's blood!" Their idea of the evening's festivities hadn't included great gobs of very red, very sticky blood.

As for Rowels, he'd no sooner hit the floor than he let out a roar like a wounded Cree, which he half was, leaped to his feet and, forgetting all about keeping one foot in front of the other, waded into his enemy with both fists going like windmills. There was a lot of power in those skinny arms, and his opponent, trying to back up to escape them, fell over backwards. With another blood-curdling scream, Rowels leaped on top of him and continued to pound him with all his might. It was quite a sight, I can tell you, with everybody on their feet and the air force screaming "Foul!" and the sailors cheering their heads off. In no time several secondary bouts had broken out between matelots and flyboys, and there was considerable consternation about.

Well, the referee finally managed to pull Rowels off his bloody opponent and the city police managed to break up the fights in the crowd. The time keeper wisely bonged on his gong and the first round was over. The second round was splendid. Rowels, realizing that a fight was a fight and to hell with all this fancy stuff, waded into his opponent and tried to kill him. He just slugged for all he was worth. Most of the blows, to be sure, landed harmlessly on arms and shoulders and even buttocks, but enough found their way to the air force lad's head to make things uncomfortable for him. But he kept flailing away, too, and by the end of the round both fighters were so tired they could hardly stand.

The third round was anticlimactic. The short rest had done nothing for either of them, and they were barely able to stagger around the ring, hugging each other and being pulled apart by the referee. The fight was finally judged a draw.

Our featherweight, Dornoski, was next up. Like Rowels, he was nervous, frightened, and determined to do his best for the honour of the navy. His best consisted of advancing to the centre of the ring with his hands held in front of him, taking a wild swing from the air force fighter and being knocked out cold.

As a matter of fact, we saw four knockouts altogether during the evening, two for us and two for them. Which may seem an inordinate number for inexperienced punchers, except that inexperience goes two ways, and none of our so-called fighters knew much about self-defence. They could duck the odd punch and pull back from a few and guard themselves to some degree, but too often they were so eager to swing at the opponent's jaw that they left themselves wide open for lucky punches. And these boys were all strong and in good condition, so that when they landed one on an unprotected jaw the result was disastrous.

But the crowd loved it, as crowds have always loved the spectacle of two individuals – be they dogs, cocks, bull and man, bear and dogs, gladiators, jousters, wrestlers or boxers – fighting to the death, or at least a reasonable facsimile. They cheered and booed and roared and, as often happens, the women became the most bloodthirsty. The sight of an otherwise demure, timid, tender, kind, loving female standing up with fire shooting out of her eyes and screaming, "Kill him! Kill him!" must surely indicate something about the human condition, but I've never been able to figure out what.

When my own fight was just about due, I stood in the dressing room with Turk Transvil. To say I was apprehensive would be a gross understatement. I was sweating like a racehorse, shaking like a nuptial bed, and fearful I would soil my baggy shorts.

"Now just remember what I told you," Turk said.

"What was that?"

"I've been telling you all week that you've got to box a fighter and fight a boxer."

"I don't even know what that means!"

"It means that this joker Rostough is a fighter, a slugger; he'll try to get in close and pound you with those short arms of his. So stay away from him. Keep him at long range."

"How am I going to do that?"

"Box him. Use your left jab. Keep jabbing him and moving to the left. Back up. Don't let him corner you."

"To quote the immortal words of Joe Louis: 'I can run, but I can't hide.' "

"You don't need to hide. Just keep the jab working. They'll give you points for those just the same as for harder punches. You're in much better shape than he is. All that road work will pay off."

I didn't tell him that most of the road work consisted of sitting in a corner ice cream parlour eating banana splits with Patricia. I wished now I'd run more. I got a bright idea.

"Why don't you go in and fight this guy? They can't call the bout off now."

"No deal. The Old Man would kill me."

"Better than Rostough killing me." But I knew it wouldn't work.

Then it was time to go. I took that long, lonely walk down the aisle through the crowd and climbed in.

As the announcer went through his silly stuff about this being the feature event of the evening, I stared across the ring at my opponent. He was big. And athletic. Joe Louis had nothing on this guy. God, but he looked strong.

Beside him I looked rather ridiculous. I'm not really built like a boxer. My arms are too long, my hands too small and my head too big. But I was nimble and fast on my feet. If I could just stay away from this brute, as Turk suggested, for three rounds and use my extra reach so that he couldn't get in close with those short, muscular arms, I might have a chance.

Thinking of this I began to think of Charlie Chaplin in *City Lights*, when he became a prizefighter to earn some money for his blind girl, and of how he managed to keep the referee between him and the other fighter all the time, dancing about as only Chaplin could. The thought of this made me laugh out loud which brought a very funny look to the face of my opponent.

"What the hell's the matter, Dink?" Smiley muttered as he dumped a sponge full of water on my head. "You feeling okay?"

"Yeah, yeah," I said. "Fine." But I couldn't help giggling. I knew a fighter was supposed to look stern and put the evil eye on his opponent, but I couldn't help it.

Somebody hit a gong and I got up to do my stuff. The other fighter advanced towards me in a crouch and so I said to myself, All right, I'll fight straight up. This guy Rostough sure looked like a slugger.

I stuck my left hand out as far as it would go and tried jabbing him with it, at the same time moving to the left. He brought up a roundhouse right that I could see coming a mile away and so I stepped back and, after it whistled by, moved in with another jab. This one caught him flush on the end of the nose and I knew it hurt him. He swung another roundhouse right and I managed to get out of the way of it, too. Well, so far so good. I'd hit him once and he hadn't hit me at all . . . so far.

Then a left came from nowhere as I was moving to the left and caught me flush on the kidney. And that hurt. So much that my arms suddenly seemed made of lead and I could hardly hold them up. So I wrapped them around my opponent, pinning his arms to his sides, and held on for dear life. The referee broke us apart and I began to back peddle for all I was worth. I had practised, as Gene Tunney said he'd done in getting ready for his second bout with Dempsey, running backwards.

The round went pretty much that way.

"Jees, Dink, you're never going to win a fight running away like that!" Smiley admonished. (He'd bet on me, too.) "You got to get in there and punch!"

I don't know what real boxers think of in the ring, but I know what I thought of. Survival. Staying alive. The essential ingredient of a boxer's makeup – the killer instinct – was entirely lacking in me. I didn't want to kill anybody. I just wanted to get out of there alive.

During the second round I got lucky. I hit him a pretty good belt in a solar plexus and to my surprise my glove sank in further than I'd expected it would. He looked a little sick for a second or two and brought his hands down and I caught him a pretty good shot to the button. This staggered him a bit and I got in a couple more before he put his short arms around me and held on. That lucky shot did me until the end of the round, when he began to come on strong again.

In the corner Smiley was ecstatic. "You've got him, Dink, you've got him! He's finished. All you have to do now is stay away from him."

To tell the truth, I felt pretty good, too. So good that I allowed myself a glance at the Old Man. And there sitting beside him in a beautiful long dress cut on the bias was none other than my true love, Patricia. That sonofabitch and Patricia! What was she thinking of? Hadn't she paid any attention to my warnings about him? Poor, sweet, innocent Patricia!

As I look back on it now I realize that even considering the sexual mores of the times and my Sunday School upbringing I was unbelievably, absurdly, disgustingly naïve.

I was still sitting there in a daze, my poor broken heart sunk down somewhere around my gym shoes, when the bell went for the third round. I still sat there.

"Get up, Dink! What the hell's wrong with you?" Smiley yelled, and pushed me off my stool into the ring.

And then I got mad. Mad at the Old Man, at Patricia, at the navy. All the frustration of the past weeks came boiling up in me and I completely lost my temper and tore into my opponent as though I'd kill him.

Here I'd dearly like to say that all this adrenalin pouring through my veins changed me into a tiger and that I knocked the stuffing out of the big air force champion. But no, truth is sadder than fiction. Everybody knows that a mad fighter is a helpless fighter if his opponent keeps his cool. I rushed at Rostough and for a while did all right, throwing rights and lefts at random. I should have been throwing them at his head. It would have worked if Rostough, like Rowels' opponent, had been a novice. But he wasn't. He simply waited for his chance and then socked me hard on the side of my head, hard enough to knock me down on the seat of my pants.

I got up all right, but all the fight was gone out of me. I hung on and ran backwards for the rest of the round, and the decision was unanimous for Rostough.

14

A Nice
Little Riot

"Jees, Dink, but your face is a mess!"

We were sitting in the beverage room of the Imperial Hotel, which was full of airmen and sailors most of whom had either won or lost money on the fights. The beer was flowing freely. Transvil was leaning over the table in the corner where about ten of us were sitting, examining my face.

"You should have boxed him, like I said."

"I should have stayed in bed." I felt terrible. Not from the bruises on my poor wounded face but from the bruises on my poor wounded heart. I had this mental picture of Patricia, back in the wardroom being pawed by the Old Man. "Frailty, thy name is woman."

"Huh? What the fug does that mean?" Dornoski asked. His face resembled mine somewhat.

"Just a quotation. Hey, have another round on me. You guys must have lost a few bucks."

"Naw. None of us had much to bet. Forget it. You done yer best."

"Anyway the Ole Man lost his hunnert bucks," somebody else said. "That's the only good thing about it."

So we sat and quaffed beer and philosophized. Some of the most taciturn guys I've known become filled with wisdom under the influence of beer.

"The way I looked at it, Dink," a tall seaman explained, "is if the Lord wanted us to be fuggin boxers we'd a bin born with fuggin boxin gloves on our fuggin hands."

Several others allowed as how that was so.

"What the fug are we using up our energy fightin the fuggin air force for anyway?" another wanted to know. "Ain't they supposed to be on our side?"

"Don't make no fuggin sense to me," another said.

"Look at it this way. We're in a war, see. We're supposed to get out and sink the German ships while those other guys shoot down their airplanes. Right?"

We all agreed that was right.

"I bet the fuggin Germans ain't usin up no energy fightin each other."

The wisdom of this was indisputable.

And so the talk went, as talk should go when people of like mind are together.

And then a navy man who had been sitting in a corner by himself getting quietly drunk got up and steered a precarious course between tables and waiters towards us. On closer inspection we could see that he was a naval officer. On still closer inspection it turned out to be Sub-Lieutenant (Special Branch) Dydell.

Now officers and ratings don't, as a rule, gather in beer parlours and shoot the breeze. And so there was a certain amount of tension in the group as Diddle slumped into a chair and splashed some beer from the glass he was carrying on the table. Nobody spoke. Finally Diddle looked up bleary-eyed and slightly bewildered at finding himself where he was. Then he shook his head as drunks will.

"You chaps certainly did your best, but we should've beat them," he muttered.

"You can say that again, sir," somebody ventured.

"It was all my fault," Diddle continued. "Don't you see, if

137

I'd stood up to the Captain, if I'd insisted, as I should have in-sisted, then we'd have had Turk in the ring against that bruiser instead of this poor, unfortunate chap here." He pointed unsteadily at me.

"Naw, it wasn't your fault, sir," Turk avowed. "We'll get them next time."

"Yeah, wait until hockey season starts. We'll show 'em," somebody else added.

"Don't you think you should go home, sir?" I said to Did-dle. I was beginning to like him better and I didn't want him to get into any trouble.

He mumbled that maybe he should, and started to get up.

It was then that Fate decided to get his grubby hand into the proceedings. From a table somewhere off to the side where a group of airmen were sitting came a loud voice saying, "Those navy jokers are all the same. Yellow. That's what's wrong with them."

Each man at our table slowly set his glass down and turned towards the offenders. But the first to speak was Diddle. In a clear voice he said, "The only difference between airmen and shit is that shit smells better."

It was so out of character that I started to laugh, but I soon stopped because things were happening.

All the waiters put down their trays of glasses and hur-ried into the middle of the floor. But it didn't matter. Sailors and airmen were slugging each other gleefully in every corner of the room. There was a beautiful sound of swearing men, breaking glass and falling tables.

I spotted Rostough at a table on the other side of the room, where he'd been acting the hero, and made for him. But Transvil got there first and, before the startled airman could get his hands up, landed a haymaker on the side of his face that could be heard across the room. I hadn't long to gloat because somebody hit me from the side and I had to attend to that.

Over near the door three airmen were pounding away at Diddle, on the theory, I suppose, that if you can't find one of your own officers to hit any officer will do. The little guy was doing a fair job of defending himself and seemed actually to be enjoying it.

And then I thought of the shore patrol. When they came the rest of us might be in some trouble all right, but for Diddle it could be disastrous. I started to move towards him but somebody knocked me over with a chair and when I got up he was gone. Through the door, I surmised, and pushed my way out.

The street seemed full of sailors, airmen, and soldiers, all swearing and hitting each other. A number of civilians attracted by the noise had joined in the fray and others were running down the sidewalk and from across the street and out of buildings to get into the action. I spotted Diddle about twenty feet away, shouting and swearing and striking out at anyone within reach. He seemed to be enjoying himself immensely. I knew that soon somebody would be using the phone and we'd be joined by a bevy of civilian and service police.

I fought my way to Diddle's side, grabbed him by the arm and heard him mutter, "What the fug are you doing?"

To hear such words coming from such refined lips so surprised me that I let go and he got away from me. Then, right beside me the big glass window of a clothing store shattered with a bang, and several people, male and female, began helping themselves to the baseball gloves, shoes, shirts and other paraphernalia. Another window was smashed and the riot was on.

Riots, like forest fires, create their own terrible momentum and now the street was jammed with crazy people, screaming, hitting, and looting. A young, flush-faced airman staggered past swigging away on a magnum of champagne and holding two more precariously under his arms. I spotted a sailor with a full case of scotch whiskey clutched in both hands and realized that someone must have broken into the liquor store that was half a block away on the other side of the street.

The entire street was jampacked with people now, and in the distance I heard the wail of a police siren. Worse, through the crowd I spotted the unmistakable white hats and webbing adorning the bodies of two immense shore patrolmen from *Porpoise.*

Where in hell was Diddle?

Then I saw him, not far away surrounded by airmen. I pushed through the crowd and shouted, "Cheez it, the cops!" as loud as I could. During the brief lull this caused, I grabbed Diddle by the arm and pulled him in an alley.

"Let go of me!" he muttered.

"Listen, you . . wh . . sir, the shore patrol gets you and your navy career is finished!"

"Fug the fuggin navy career!"

In desperation I yanked him along the alley where it was pitch dark but where at least there were no combatants. I felt my way along a brick wall hauling Diddle after me, and now I realized another problem. Not being accustomed to drink, Diddle was about to pass out so that I was more dragging than leading him.

Then I ran into another brick wall. A blind alley! We were trapped. Frantically I felt along the wall and came to a doorknob, turned it and a door opened. I pulled Diddle inside and shoved the door shut. From the smell I realized there was a kitchen nearby and that we had come in through the back door of a café on the next street.

I pushed Diddle along the passageway towards a dim light, which when we got there turned out to be over a door marked WOMEN. I shoved open the door with my elbow and pulled Diddle inside. Luckily there were no women in the tiny room, but how long would it be before one came? I propped Diddle up on the throne, ran some water into the small grubby basin and dipped a towel into it. With this I splashed cold water on his face and hissed, "Keep awake, Lieutenant! We've got to get out of here!" He mumbled some profanity but didn't fall off the throne.

Somehow I had to disguise him. He still had on his naval cap with the officer's insignia about the peak, and his jacket with the stripes on the sleeves. I took off the hat and shoved it under my jersey, pulled off his jacket and folded it inside out over my arm. Now he could pass, temporarily, for a civilian in blue pants and white shirt with a starched collar and tie. Then I heard footsteps coming down the corridor. If they were some woman wanting to use the facilities I was finished. But the footsteps went by.

Carefully I opened the door, pulled Diddle through, and hurried him down the hall towards the front of the café. There were a few customers at some scruffy tables and a couple sitting at the counter. The counterman, who obviously doubled as cashier, had his back to us, pouring hot water into a large aluminum container with a tap on the bottom, used in those days for making coffee. I pulled Diddle past him and out the front door to an almost deserted street. From the next street I could hear the sound of crashing glass, cursing men, screaming women and police sirens. The riot was in full swing.

Then my luck improved. Coming down the street was a car with a little rectangular light on top. I shouted and the taxi pulled over to the curb. I opened the door and shoved Diddle inside.

"Where to, bud?" the taxi driver asked.

Where indeed? Certainly not back to the ship. I shook Diddle to ask him where he lived, but he was dead to the world. I shook him again. Still no response. So I slapped him as hard as I could. Striking officers was becoming a bad habit.

"What's the idea?" the cabbie enquired over his shoulder.

"Nothing. Just drive to the other side of town. I'll tell you where."

So he drove and I finally got Diddle's address out of him and got him to his boarding house and into bed.

The next day, I knew, would be bad.

15

You're Driving
Me Crazy

The next day was indeed bad. There was a decided pall of gloom over the ship when I went aboard. Lightson had a grim look on his face, and after morning exercises about twenty ratings were on the quarterdeck for disciplinary action.

I thought for once I'd got out of it until, after the quarterdeck session, Lightson summoned me.

"The Captain wants to see you."

"Me? Why me?"

"You're so damned innocent. But your halo is a bit tattered. It just so happens that the Captain has a pretty good idea who really started the fight that led to last night's riot."

Diddle? Then all my efforts had been, as they say, for naught.

I didn't say anything and Lightson ushered me into the forecastle and into the Captain's office. I wasn't sure whether or not I should take off my cap, but noticing that he still had his on, decided to wear mine until given an Off Cap order by Lightson, who was standing by looking very stern indeed.

"Well, Diespecker," the Old Man said, leaning back in his swivel chair. "You've done it again."

"Sir?"

"Starting a disturbance that got this ship's company into disfavour with the city authorities, at a time when our relations had a chance of reaching an all-time high."

"Me?"

"Do you deny you were with the group at the Imperial Hotel?"

"No, but . . ."

"Do you deny that you made a remark that started the fight?"

"Yes, sir, I do."

"Then who did?"

"I can't say, sir. I don't remember."

The Captain glanced at Lightson, who nodded ever so slightly. "There seems to be a complete loss of memory in everyone involved. Well, what have you got to say for yourself?"

Trying to think fast and cunningly with a head full of mush isn't easy. "One of the airmen made disparaging remarks about the navy, sir."

"What remarks?"

"He said we were fuggin yellow."

"And you think you aren't." He leaned heavily on the "you" and I knew he was thinking of the hundred bucks he'd lost.

"I didn't mind for myself, sir, but I couldn't let them impute the honour of the naval service." Somehow I knew this was the line to take.

The Old Man sort of smiled slightly and then said, "How long have you been around here, Diespecker?"

"Too long, sir. I missed the first draft."

"How did you manage to do that?"

Here it was again. Damn his rotten hide anyway. "I had nothing to do with it, sir. My name was left off the draft list is all." I glanced over at Lightson when I said this and so did the Old Man, but I could see he wasn't going to ask any questions in that quarter.

143

But I'd started now and I wasn't about to quit. "May I say something, sir?"

"Go ahead."

"I did well in all my tests. I've learned everything there is to know around here and I can't understand why I missed the draft. If I'm not on the next one, sir, I'd like to have a discharge and try one of the other services."

By the way the Old Man stiffened in his chair I knew I'd gone too far. "I should say you have been around here too long, Diespecker!" he shouted. "You've become a regular sea lawyer. Well, let me tell you, the only discharge you'll get from here is a dishonourable discharge, and then no other service will take you. Understand?"

"Yes, sir." Damn, I'd blown it.

"But I'm not going to give you a dishonourable discharge. Your conduct doesn't warrant it. You are confined to barracks for the next two weeks to perform such duties as Chief Petty Officer Lightson deems suitable."

That was the end of it. Almost. Lightson bellowed at me to "About turn," but before I was marched off the Old Man gave his parting shot.

"As to whether or not you'll leave here with the next draft depends entirely on yourself. If Chief Petty Officer Lightson deems that you are worthy to represent the navy, you'll be drafted out. Otherwise you'll damned well stay here until you are!"

We left, and now it was Lightson's turn. "So, Smartass, it didn't work."

I knew better than to talk back to Lightson.

"I suppose you knew that the Captain had a hundred bucks bet on you in that fight."

Still no answer.

"But not me. I knew better than to put down any money on you."

I was indulging in a little fantasy then. In this fantasy Lightson and I were meeting in civilian life. No uniforms, no K.R. and A.I., just two guys. The fantasy was beautiful, so beautiful that I smiled to myself. This infuriated Lightson more.

"Okay, you heard what the Old Man said. 'Any duties that Chief Petty Officer Lightson deems suitable.' Well right now I deem it suitable that you should clean out the heads. Mop up all the piss on the floor. Scour all the shit stains from the bowels. Clean the urinals. Scrub all the graffiti off the walls. Now hop to it. Smartly!"

I hopped to it smartly.

The first night of my punishment, when I was on my knees holystoning the deck of the recreation room for, to my certain knowledge, the eighteenth time since I joined the ship, Sub-Lieutenant (Special Branch) Dydell came into the room.

I jumped to my feet as any good rating should do at the approach of an officer and a gentleman. This confused him and he muttered, "At ease. Or whatever."

I at eased. Diddle looked absolutely awful. Gone was the spit and polish and the primness and the dedicated look of the scoutmaster. There was something about the look in his eyes that I liked.

"What happened to me last night at the Imperial?" he asked.

"Don't you remember?"

"I remember going into the Imperial beer parlour." He rubbed his forehead miserably. "But then I can't remember anything else. Is that possible?"

"I've had complete blackouts. Yes."

He shook his head in bewilderment. "Do you know that's the first time I've ever been drunk in my life? I was so mad at the Captain. Imagine his letting the air force pull a stunt like that." He was getting all worked up again so I thought I'd better stop it.

"Everything's crazy around here!"

He regarded me for a moment with his bleary eyes. "Yes, I think you're right. I really do. But what about you?"

"Don't worry about me. I've been in shit so much I'm beginning to smell like it. Can't last forever."

"I admired the way you went into that bout. Overmatched as you were. I should have stood up to the Old Man and prevented it."

"What the hell. I might have won if I hadn't blown my cool."

He was rubbing his forehead again. He sat down on the rumpled old couch and invited me to do the same.

"You know," he said after a while in an awed voice. "I learned something last night."

"What was that, sir?"

"It may be a good thing to get drunk once in a while. Sort of relieves the tension."

"That's what they say."

"I've always thought of alcohol as an unmitigated evil. But maybe, maybe, well, it sort of clears the head in a funny way."

"I've found that to be so."

He heaved himself to his feet, still shaking his head. "I sure wish I could remember. What did I do during the riot?"

"I really don't remember, sir. I was too busy protecting myself. Besides, I was drunker than you."

With that he left.

Was he telling the truth about the blackout? I'm sure he was. In any case, I had made a good friend, and as it turned out, I was going to need all the good friends I could get.

One late afternoon when I was polishing brass in the recreation room, Lightson sent his bumboy to find me.

"Lightson wants you," he simpered.

"What for?"

"How should I know? He just said to report to his office on the double."

"Oh, shit."

I reported more or less on the double and Lightson was actually smiling.

"Got a job for you tonight, Deeespecker. One you might like."

Beware of C.P.O.s bearing gifts.

"Oh?"

"The Old Man has to go somewhere in the car and his

146

regular driver has shore leave. You'll be his driver for the evening."

"What about the recreation room floor?"

"It'll keep. Now get yourself cleaned up. Shave. And put on your dress uniform, and when you're driving the Old Man don't run into anything."

Lightson was enjoying this too much. Driving the big, black navy sedan was a great improvement over waxing floors, but why should it please Lightson to give me a half-decent job?

"Pick him up at his hotel at nineteen hundred. Now get out of here."

At exactly seven o'clock, civilian time, I pulled up to the curb in front of the Evereen Hotel, a small, first-class hotel on Duke Street that catered to long-staying guests. The Old Man came out the door as I drove up.

He was wearing his dress uniform and looked pretty swanky. I stood at attention beside the open back door and saluted. He returned the salute without looking at me and got in.

"Twenty-one Rosewood Crescent," he said.

Twenty-one Rosewood Crescent! Patricia's address! Now I understood the smug look on Lightson's face.

At Patricia's house I again sprang out and opened the door for him and again he didn't look at me. After a short wait he and Patricia came out of the house, and, oh my, she did look great. Long dress, short fox fur, high heels. My gut did a flip-flop just looking at her.

But she didn't look at me any more than the Old Man had. (I should mention here that although he was referred to as the Old Man he couldn't have been more than thirty-five years old. Oh for the days when thirty-five seemed old.) They got in the back as cozy as could be. The Old Man said, "Colonial Hotel," and I wheeled off down the street. I knew then they were going to attend a dinner dance for which the hotel was famous. Dining and dancing. Ah me.

So for about ten blocks I was treated to the kind of conversation a guy uses when he's trying to make it with his date. Just little inconsequential remarks and titterings and the rest.

147

When I pulled up at the front door and let them out, the Old Man said, "Be back at eleven, driver, and wait for us," and away they sashayed through the entrance.

So I had about three and a half hours to kill. I drove straight for the Imperial Hotel on the east side, parked my limousine and headed for the beer parlour.

Naturally Smiley and a half dozen other sailors were there, and when Smiley saw me he shouted, "Hey, here's a guy I want to buy a drink for," and ordered the waiter to line up half a dozen glasses in front of me. I began drinking at an inordinate rate, and the more I drank the soberer I became and the madder I got.

"How come you pulled driver duty?" Smiley asked. "After the Old Man lost a hundred big ones on you I'd think he'd never want to set eyes on you again."

"He hasn't. Lightson assigned me to the duty."

"But he hates you even more than the Old Man does."

"I know. Popularity kid, that's me. But Lightson had his own diabolical motive in this. You see, the Old Man took my girl to the Colonial dinner dance."

"What?" It came from all around the table.

"The Old Man doesn't know I'm his driver," I added. "And neither does Patricia. They're so damned busy with each other they haven't even looked at me yet."

This piece of information elicited some head shaking and some ripe remarks.

"What are you going to do?" Smiley wanted to know.

"There are several possibilities. I could go back to the ship and get a service revolver and shoot them both. That has dramatic overtones that I rather like."

"It would also get your neck stretched," somebody suggested.

"Or I could run the car off the Queen Street bridge and drown the three of us."

"Impractical," Smiley said. "In the first place, the concrete railings are too high and too strong, and the water isn't deep enough to drown anybody."

"I know," a little rating with a face like a gopher shouted

enthusiastically, "aim the car at a post, see, and just before she hits, jump out. Then they'll both be killed, but you'll have had a miraculous escape!"

I gave this careful consideration as I sipped my fourth beer, but finally abandoned it because I really didn't want to kill Patricia. Just the Old Man.

Smiley was worried. "This could be real bad for you, Dink. Smarner, the Old Man's regular driver, has got some sort of deal with him. He'll never say a word about where he takes him or anything else. I've put out some subtle feelers to find out, but he's absolutely close-mouthed. Besides, he doesn't drink." Then his face clouded. "I'll bet anything you want that the Old Man thinks Smarner's driving him tonight. You two are about the same build," he added, sizing me up.

"Who cares?"

"You'd better. And don't let the Captain see your face, Dink. Don't say nothing. That's the way Smarner is. Never opens his mouth. I know that."

I sort of lost track of time then so that when I had to leave and pick up the Old Man and my girl I had downed eight glasses of beer.

Sitting in front of the hotel, I was in that nice fuzzy condition when you don't think about what's going to happen and you don't care much. About half an hour later the big glass doors swung open and into the crisp night air emerged the Old Man and the love of my life.

At once I could see that he was high and she was low. He'd obviously been into the booze since they got there, and I guessed Patricia had drunk practically nothing. Out of the car I sprang and opened the door, keeping my head lowered as I'd seen Smarner do. I saluted but the Old Man didn't return it; just hustled her into the back seat.

"Just drive around a bit," he instructed. "Take it easy."

From then on, as I wheeled slowly down River Drive, the dialogue from the back seat went something like this:

PATRICIA: I really should be getting home, sir.

O.M.: Nonsense, my dear. The night is young. And please, my name is Austin.

PATRICIA: I really have had a wonderful time, uh, Austin, but –

O.M.: I'm so glad to hear you say that, my dear. Because I have had a smashing time. You know there is something so refreshing about you western girls, so fresh, and honest, and, uh . . . generous.

PATRICIA: Aren't eastern girls all those things?

O.M.: Oh, good heavens, no. Entirely different. You can't imagine how wonderful it is to me to be with you after . . . well . . . my wife.

ME (to myself): She doesn't understand you.

O.M.: You see, she doesn't understand me. Oh I know she tries, but she's so caught up with her bridge club and her Cancer Society work and the Junior League and, well, we've drifted apart.

ME (to myself): Should have brought my violin.

PATRICIA (eagerly): I worked for the Cancer Society once.

O.M. (bored): Indeed.

PATRICIA: I thought it was the most stimulating experience. Yes, I really did. You see they had this campaign to raise funds for research and other things, but mostly for research. Do you know that we have some of the best cancer researchers in Canada, in the world, right here at the university? They've done such marvellous things. For instance –

O.M.: When you cross the bridge, driver, go up to the University Park. It's so beautiful there and, uh, quiet.

PATRICIA: No, please . . .

But I had already turned the corner and was driving up the dark street into the darker University Park. From the back seat I could hear propositions and protests, both becoming more urgent by the minute.

O.M.: One little kiss won't hurt.

ME (to myself): If she says she's not that kind of girl, I'll scream.

PATRICIA: I'm not that kind of girl. Really, Austin. Austin, please stop! You mustn't!

There was more of this. It sounded something like a wrestling match in the back and I was beginning to wonder what the penalty for killing an officer really was.

There was a circular drive in front of Convocation Hall and back between the buildings was a jungle of lilac, forsythia, and other shrubs; and in among the shrubs a number of twisting paths which were well known to undergraduates who, during varsity dances, were wont to take their dates there for a bit of dalliance.

"Stop here," the Old Man instructed and I stopped. "Take a walk, driver," he went on. "And don't hurry back."

What to do? Patricia was protesting, but her protests were becoming weaker, through sheer fatigue, I guessed. I got out of the car and of course when I opened my door the inside light came on and I could see the dear girl practically engulfed by this lusting brute. Then, not knowing what else to do, I opened the back door, too. In bewilderment the Old Man sort of let go, allowing Patricia to squirm out of his grasp and spring lightly out of the car.

"Damn!" The Old Man climbed out, not so lightly. "Where are you going?"

"Catch me!" the girl giggled and like a will-o-the-wisp in white muslin disappeared down one of the paths. The Old Man lumbered after her and I sprinted after him, the difference between us being that he knew what he'd do if he caught her but I was damned if I knew what I'd do if I caught him.

Patricia seemed to know the paths – perhaps she'd been there before – and she actually seemed to be enjoying the game. I could hear her light laughter coupled with the Old Man's heavy footsteps and gasping curses. It was no contest of course. She was young and lithe and in good condition from all the tennis she played. He was fifteen years older, getting thick around the middle and badly out of shape.

Knowing Patricia was safe, I gave up the chase and soon the Old Man did, too. He dragged himself back to the car gasping for breath and cursing loudly. It was obvious that even if she were willing now he was too pooped to participate. I held the door for him, and still not looking at me, he slumped into the back seat.

Patricia came back, too, and from her bearing it seemed to me that she was a little disappointed that the chase was over. I stood there holding the door open, feeling a little like St. George must have felt after he'd rescued the maiden from the dragon. I don't know what kind of thanks St. George got, but Patricia's voice was strangely petulant as she recognized me.

"Robin! What in the world are you doing here?"

This brought the Old Man to life and, leaning out the door, he roared, "Diespecker! You! Where the hell is Smarner?"

"On leave, sir. Chief Petty Officer Lightson assigned me this duty. I've tried to carry it out to the best of my ability, sir." And suddenly I realized I had the Old Man cold. I was just carrying out orders.

Patricia didn't say anything, but got into the back seat beside him.

"Oh hell!" the Old Man grunted and I actually felt a little sorry for him. "Drive us to Miss Reilly's home."

And that's what I did. As I drove away from her house the Old Man started to chew me out, but I intercepted him.

"I understand, sir, that Smarner is a most discreet driver. Never gossips about what happens. I think this is an admirable quality."

"Oh, you do? So you're not above a little blackmail?"

"I don't understand what you mean, sir."

"Well, you'll find out, Diespecker. You'll find out."

I drove him back to his hotel and let him out, saluting smartly as I did so.

I guess when he sobered up and realized the position he'd be in if I blabbed to the men, he decided to go along with our unwritten agreement.

But that was the only time I ever drove the Old Man anywhere.

16

For the Prevention of Disease Only

Three things happened as a direct result of my evening as the Captain's driver.

My relations with the Old Man stabilized. He seemed to hate me as much as ever, but by the terms of our little deal he couldn't do anything overt about it. However, as I was to learn, you never win a fight with a policeman or a C.O.

My relationship with Lightson deteriorated badly. Since he had to hit at somebody and couldn't, for the time being at least, hit at me, the Old Man took it out on Lightson, and Lightson took it out on me. He thought up new refinements on the foul-up-Diespecker campaign. It seemed to me that whenever anything good was happening to the ship's company I was left out, and when anything bad was happening I was right in the middle of it.

My relations with Patricia greatly improved. She sent a message through my brother, Doug. Doug came down to the ship, sauntered in through the side door and found me chipping a mixture of paint and grease and oil and dirt off a bulkhead.

"Is this all you ever do?" he asked.

"What do you want?"

153

"Got a message for you."

"Stuff it."

"From Patricia."

"What? What is it?"

"I've stuffed it."

It took some time and no small amount of bribery to get Doug to divulge his message, which was that I was invited to Patricia's home for dinner the following Sunday. Since my last day of Number Eleven would be over on Saturday, I gleefully told Doug to phone Patricia and tell her I'd be there.

So I was in pretty high spirits when I headed for her house that Sunday afternoon. My mind was full of all sorts of little plans, but none of them included what I was later to be accused of.

On the way out of the barracks I was handed a little package of condoms. This had become standard procedure, since so many of the boys from the country had found the flesh pots of the city so much to their liking they had picked up what are politely called "social diseases." So Doc had issued orders that everybody going ashore or on leave or whatever should be well equipped for whatever eventuality might arise.

This, by the way, had led to one of the more bizarre scenes that I remember from HMCS *Porpoise*. A Russian movie was playing at a theatre on the east side of the city, called, I think, *The Defence of Stalingrad*. And since the Russians were at that time our bosom pals and staunch allies and all around good guys, the whole ship's company was detailed to see the picture. Instead of marching us there, they loaded us on a streetcar and away we went. To while away the time during the journey some of the ratings took to blowing up their special issues to enormous sizes, three feet long at least, tying off the ends and releasing them out the windows on an unsuspecting public, shouting, "Away depth charges!" As we passed a school that was just going in after recess, about thirty of the great ballons sailed out on the street, and the children eagerly gathered them up to take to their teachers for show and tell.

But I digress. Where was I? Oh yes, on the way to

Patricia's house. It was a fine house surrounded by shrubbery and a fence, as befitted the station of the doctor who lived there.

Dr. William Reilly, Patricia's father, was tall and dignified, with a fine head of hair, a pronounced chin and spectacles that had neither frames nor shafts, but clamped on the nose. He was formally dressed in a dark suit, and he spoke in a deep voice full of authority. I was terrified of him and he was suspicious of me.

Like a lot of fathers, he had the idea that sailors were up to no good where their daughters were concerned. Besides, Patricia's dating patterns were somewhat confusing; first a C.O. and now a rating. His wife, a small, buxom woman, was a bit more relaxed, and Patricia's little sister Susie was so relaxed that she crawled all over me, and kept asking me questions like, "How many submarines have you sunk?"

As we sat down to dinner at the beautiful oak dining table, the Reillys one at each end, me on one side and Patricia and Susie across from me, I became even more nervous. To tell the truth, I had never in my life sat at such an elegant table in such elegant surroundings. Despite meat rationing, Mrs. Reilly had managed to get a fine standing rib roast, which the good doctor proceeded to carve with a silver-handled carving knife.

"Rare or medium?" he boomed at me.

"Huh? I mean, pardon?"

"Your meat. Would you prefer a rare slice, a medium slice or a well-done slice?"

This was a situation I had never before encountered. My father always dished out the meat as it came to hand.

"Oh, whatever's handiest," I said.

"I assure you it's all very handy, right here in front of me. Which do you prefer?"

"Uh, well-done, please, sir."

Whereupon he made a face like a surgeon who has come upon an appendix on the wrong side, and laboriously turned the roast around, giving me the impression that anyone who preferred his meat well-done was a slob indeed. But he cut me a good-sized slice, put in on a plate and passed it to his wife who was handling the vegetables.

With spoon poised, she asked, "Sprouts or carrots?"

"Pardon?"

"Would you prefer Brussel sprouts or creamed carrots?"

I'd never heard of Brussel sprouts, but carrots we grew aplenty. "Oh, carrots, please." It seemed like an awful lot of fuss just to load a plate with food, but finally it was accomplished and we got down to eating.

I had been a little apprehensive that the good doctor would quiz me some about my naval career to date, but I needn't have worried.

"I was in the first show, you know," he informed me between bites of roast.

"Huh?"

"The first war, in France, you know. I was with the First Battalion medical team. I'd just finished my internship at Toronto General. No, by George, I wasn't quite finished, when they snapped up the entire class for service in the field."

"That must have been interesting." A piece of creamed carrot had slid off my plate when I was cutting my meat and I was trying to get it back on again without anybody seeing.

"Interesting! I should say. There I was not much older than you when they started bringing the wounded in. I can tell you my surgical education was accelerated a hundredfold. The very first man I saw had taken a piece of shrapnel in the abdomen and his entire –"

"Please, William," Mrs. Reilly interrupted. "Not while we are eating."

"Yes, yes, of course. I tried to get into this show, too, but the old ticker isn't what it used to be. Of course, I can still play eighteen holes of golf every day. Do you golf?"

"No."

"Any sports?"

"Just baseball and hockey." I didn't mention the boxing. But Susie did.

"He was in that boxing match they had at the arena," she piped. "He got clobbered."

"Indeed? Fine sport, boxing. We had some great boxers with the First. But the thing I remember best was when the Dumbell troupe came to entertain. You've heard of them?"

"Yes, I've seen them at the old Empire Theatre, when I was a kid."

"Not the same thing at all. These were the men in the trenches. Soldiers all. Captain Plunkett was the man who organized them." He started to sing "Oh, oh, oh it's a lovely war . . ." "Ah those were great times!"

"Great times, sir? But I thought you said –"

"Oh, they were bad times, too, make no mistake about that. But there is something about the army – and the navy, too, I daresay – the comradeship, the *esprit de corps*."

He had a far away, dreamy look on his face, as though those army years were the best of his entire life. His wife obviously didn't share this feeling.

Somehow I got through that meal without using the wrong fork or upsetting anything, and I was feeling not too bad near the finish, when disaster struck.

Throughout the meal Patricia had said very little. How could she with that gabby father? And I, when I wasn't trying to pay attention to the ex-army surgeon, just sort of stared at her. She was so, well, delicious. I can't remember now whether Patricia was what you'd call beautiful or not – any more than that all girls of eighteen are beautiful. They are so fresh and dainty and coy and so damned flirtatious. She sat there across the table from me, giving me these occasional little glances and smiles and reducing me to jelly.

To this day I don't know what she really thought of me then, whether she was attracted or not. The point is, I was there and I was male and I was young, the only young male within reach, and so I became the target for her cute little gestures, pursing of the lips, batting of the lashes, tossing of the hair. I was in love, good old-fashioned ga-ga in love, a patsy, a sitting duck, utterly helpless.

But I was doing all right, too. With that intuition that all females possess, Patricia's mother had sensed my condition. I don't see how she could miss it. Also, she was probably on my side as she couldn't have been too happy about her daughter dating the Old Man. And so she was being very kind. Perhaps she remembered when that boring, pompous, egotistical, self-satisfied ass at the other end of the table was young and in love with her. Anyway, for whatever reason, she smiled sweetly at me and asked me questions about myself.

"How did you come to choose the navy?"

"Uh, I've always had the idea I'd like to be a sailor."

"Were there any sailors in your family?"

"No. Not that I ever heard of. Actually, the biggest vessel I've ever been on was a raft we made when I was twelve and launched on a slough just out of town. It sank."

"Aren't you afraid you'll be seasick?"

"No. I think they've got pills for that now."

And so on and so on. While she quizzed me she was serving the dessert, which consisted of chocolate cake and ice cream. It's difficult to eat chocolate cake and ice cream at any time, but doubly difficult when one is trying to field questions, keep from belching and prevent his table napkin from sliding off his knee onto the floor. The first two I managed, but not the third.

The damned thing just disappeared. I don't know why table napkins do that, but I've always had trouble with them. They just slide off and disappear.

And then I managed somehow to get my fingers covered with a mixture of ice cream and chocolate icing. So there I was, squirming and fretting and trying to peer down between my legs to find my napkin and answer questions about what I thought it would be like to be in the middle of the North Atlantic in a gale.

Then I remembered that I had a handkerchief. Now there are no pockets in what we called a round rig uniform. Instead there is a money belt for what money a sailor might have, while cigarette packages and various other sundries are stuffed down in the front of the jersey, in much the way that women keep things down between their breasts. So, completely reduced to jelly by this time, I frantically fished into my bosom, found the end of the handkerchief and pulled it out. It came out all right, but so, too, did my forgotten envelope of condoms. It performed a neat little parabola and landed with a plop in Mrs. Reilly's cup of coffee.

I will draw the veil of silence over the rest of this dismal scene. I didn't remain long in the Reilly household after the conclusion of the meal. I detected an air of aloofness in the entire family, as a matter of fact. And as I trudged down the front steps of that fine house into the brisk November evening I felt about as low as a man can feel.

But, as some radio comic of my youth was wont to remark, I hadn't seen anything yet.

17

Leave for Sam

And so the lousy war dragged on. In London German bombs battered buildings and bodies. In Paris German bullies swaggered and tortured. In the North Atlantic German submarines blasted merchant ships while Canadian corvettes bobbed like corks beside the convoys, hunting the wolf packs with radar and belabouring them with depth charges. In Wabagoon, becoming more frustrated with each passing day, I fought a losing battle with Lieutenant Commander Featherby and Chief Petty Officer Lightson.

But there were troubles greater than mine.

One Saturday morning when I was scrubbing and waxing the office floors, a job that never got properly done no matter how much muscle I applied, Smiley came in looking like a fifth columnist.

After he was sure nobody was lurking under any desks, he beckoned me closer.

"Hey, Dink."

"Yeah?"

"Sam's back."

"Sam? Oh Sam! Great! He got leave. Where is he?"

"Not so bloody loud, you fool! He didn't get leave. He went over the hill."

"Huh?"

"Deserted."

"Jesus! What would he do a thing like that for?"

"That damned wife of his. She's shacking up with some draft dodger."

"Damn! Have you seen Sam? Where is he?"

"I haven't seen him and I don't know where he is. But a signal came through on him. Writer Donner told me about it. The shore patrol was instructed to keep an eye open for him."

"What'll they do if they catch him?"

"Throw him in the brig, I guess. Maybe worse. Dishonourable discharge. The works. Unless – "

"Unless what?"

"We can find him and persuade him to give himself up. Then he'd just get hit with being absent without leave." He took off his cap and ran a hand through his thinning hair. "That bitch Gertie. Drawing her allowance and getting most of his pay and then she does a thing like that!"

"Yeah. Well, we tried to warn the crazy bugger, but there was no way he wasn't going to get married. We better go looking for him."

"Yeah. When are you off?"

"Tomorrow."

"Okay. We go up there together. I can get the address from Donner. But for chrissake don't tell anybody about this!"

"Gee, I'm glad you told me that. I was just about to go to my pal, Lieutenant Commander Featherby, and ask his advice."

"Go to hell."

"Tomorrow."

The next morning we went looking for Gertrude. We found her in a crummy flat over on the east side. Up three flights with a powerful stench of cooking and rot that must have been lingering in the halls for years. Places like that and smells like that always depress me terribly. For it is the stench of poverty and misguidedness and bad luck and all their attending evils.

We found the apartment at the top of a long flight of steps that led to the third floor. A flimsy railing ran along the side of the stair well and I remember thinking how easy it would be to fall down the thirty or so feet to the floor below.

We knocked on the door of 301 and waited. From inside came the mutterings of two voices. Was one of them male? We knocked again and after a little wait the door was opened as far as the night chain would allow it to go. A blonde head peeked around the door.

"Hi, Gertie," I said, quietly. "It's me, Dink Diespecker. Is Sam here?"

She moved over a little then and I saw she was wearing a slip with no dress over it, a slip that did a poor job of holding up her heavy breasts. She was alarmed.

"Sam? No. For Christ sake he's off in St. Hyacinthe. Ain't he?"

"That's where he's supposed to be, all right," Smiley said. "But he isn't. He went over the hill."

"What?" Now she wasn't alarmed; she was scared. "Why in hell would he do a thing like that?"

"Damned if we know. Do you?" Smiley's voice was sharp.

"Jees. If some dirty bastard has been telling him lies about me –"

"What kind of lies?"

"Never you mind. He ain't here!"

"Well, if he comes here, you'd better tell him to give himself up. He's in big trouble already, but he could be in a lot bigger."

"Oh God. That stupid hick."

"That's your loving husband you're referring to, I presume." Smiley was losing control.

"Mind your own goddamned business!" The door shut with a bang.

"That bitch. That bitch. That bitch!" Smiley's face was white as paper. "She's got somebody in there with her right now."

"Yeah. Come on. Let's go. We'd better find Sam before he comes here."

I found Sam, all right, or rather he found me. Smiley and I had been having a few in the beer parlour of the Imperial, for, as Smiley sagaciously pointed out, "If that big bugger comes to town, this is one place he'll come looking for us."

"Think he'll come to town?"

"Bound to. Sooner or later. If he makes it, that is, with every shore patrol in the country looking for him. They'll soon go to see Gertie, you can be sure of that."

And so, in the interest of finding Sam, we spent considerable time at the Imperial and consumed considerable glasses of draft beer. It was one of those rare times when Lightson hadn't found anything to hit me with and so my evenings were my own.

This night, a cold windy one, I remember, with a bitter wind blowing dead leaves along the streets and the temperature almost freezing, I'd left Smiley at the door of the beer parlour and caught the last streetcar home.

I had a half block to walk to the house from the streetcar stop and I had the collar of my great coat turned up and was holding my gloved hands in front of my face for protection from the wind. I was just turning up our walk when a figure detached itself from behind a box elder tree on the boulevard and hissed my name.

"Hey, Dink!"

"What? Is that you, Sam?"

"Yeah. I been waiting for you for over an hour."

"Where the hell have you been?" Then I saw his teeth were chattering with the cold. "Come on in the house. Everybody's in bed. But for God sake keep quiet!"

I knew I was committing a naval misdemeanour or crime far worse than the penny-ante stuff I'd been charged with up to now. But what else could I do?

We went up the veranda steps and in through the glassed-in porch and I pushed the front door open. Right away from upstairs came my mother's voice.

"Robin, is that you?"

163

My mother never slept a wink until everybody in the family was accounted for. No matter how late it was when I came in, I'd hear, "Robin, is that you?"

I know that if there is such a place as heaven and I happen to make it there when I'm dead, the first thing I'll hear when they open those pearly gates is my mother asking, "Robin, is that you?" And then, when I've assured her I'm in, will come the next inevitable line. "It's awful late, you know. Where have you been?"

This was a rhetorical question, I knew, and I never bothered answering it, realizing that she'd be right off to sleep when I answered her first question.

It was cold in the house. Dad always let the furnace go way down because we were supposed to save coal. The trains that normally carried it from Alberta to our place were busy elsewhere carrying young men to their appointment with adventure.

Sam and I sat in the big kitchen. I poked the range and there were still coals in it. A few sticks of wood got it blazing and I set the big brass kettle on the open hole above the flames.

"I'll make us some tea."

"Are you sure nobody'll come down?" Sam asked.

He had the air of a hunted stag about him. Head drawn down into the open neck of his ragged shirt, eyes darting from side to side. I don't know where he'd picked up the civilian clothes, but they were awful. A dirty old pair of trousers with holes in the knees. Somebody's discarded oxfords with holes in the soles. A flimsy windbreaker that had seen much better days. He was so cold he kept giving those long shuddering sobs.

"Okay, friend," I said. "What happened?"

"Got a cigarette?"

"Yeah, sure." I gave him one and he lit it with a trembling hand, leaning on the old oilcloth-covered kitchen table. Sitting on one of our old wooden chairs, as old at least as I was, he sucked in the smoke and it seemed to help him control the shudders.

"This guy – remember him? – Womsby, a stoker?"

"I kind of remember him. Red hair and freckles."

"Yeah, that's him. Well, he got leave to come home. Compassionate leave, they called it, because his brother in the air force was killed in a training accident. Anyway, he got leave. Maybe you heard about it?"

"No, don't remember hearing. What about him?"

"Well, he came back to base and he said he'd seen . . . seen Gertie with this guy and said everybody knew she was going out with him." Sam sucked in his breath and his lean jaw began to twitch just below his ear. "That he was living with her . . . in the rooms she was renting with the money I sent her."

"So what did you do?"

"I almost went crazy. My Gertie and another guy? I didn't believe it, honest to God I didn't, but I had to find out. So I phoned her."

"What did she say?"

He looked at me like a hurt horse. "She told me to go fugg myself. Then she hung up. Jesus!" He sat there and there were tears in his eyes. He hadn't touched the tea I'd made him or the bread and cheese.

"So what did you do then?"

"Well, I put in for this compassionate leave, same as Womsby got. Finally got to talk to the Number One at the base and he sent me to see the padre." Sam rubbed his big hand over his big face. The memory of the padre, I could see, was not good. He shook his head, remembering. "The padre. Minister of the gospel. What's he in the navy for anyway? To help people?"

"Or put the fear of God into them."

"Yeah. Well, he did that all right. Should have heard him. You'd think I'd committed a crime. Sat there and lectured me about the sins of the modern generation as though I was responsible for all of them. Shucks, I haven't even got any sins. Or didn't have then."

"He turned down your request?"

"Flat. I tried to convince him, but all he could see was that I wanted some time off. If he'd just given me that compassionate leave." It was a cry of pain.

Sam started to get up.

"Where are you going?" I asked.

"Home."

"In a pig's patoot you are. That place will be swarming with shore patrol!"

"Then where?"

"Stay here. Sleep with me tonight. Nobody needs to know. I'll tell Ma that you're a friend who needed a place to put up for the night. She's used to it. Before the war it happened often enough. And you stay in the room. I'm too tired and too hung over to think straight now. Tomorrow I'll come up with something."

But the next morning I came up empty. I left Sam in my room and told him to go down and get some breakfast after Doug had gone to school.

Before I went out I told Ma that Sam was in town to enlist but had no place to stay and he'd be here for a couple of days. She said that would be okay. I high-tailed it down to HMCS *Porpoise*.

At morning Stand Easy I got hold of Smiley.

"Jees," he said, "you look like you were up all night."

"I was. With Sam."

"What?"

"Not so loud."

"Where is he?"

"Never mind. You don't know anything about it, see. No use us both being in trouble. One is bad enough. You don't even know I've seen him."

"Correct."

"But you've got to give me some advice. What should I do?"

Smiley thought this over carefully. "He's got to give himself up."

"What? Where?"

"Right here. Tell him to shave and get a haircut and get all cleaned up, with his uniform pressed. He's still got his uniform?"

"Don't know. He was in some beat-up civies."

"He'll have it. Get all dressed up neat and come in and give himself up to the duty officer. Tonight it's Lieutenant Walton. A good guy."

"What will happen to him?"

"He'll get rapped for being AWOL. But like I said, if he doesn't give himself up and the shore patrol or the civilian cops pick him up he's a deserter. Dishonourable discharge. Jail. The works."

"You're sure?"

"Course I'm sure, for chrissake. Not only that, but it stays with you the rest of your life. Like being in the pen. Dishonourable discharge would ruin Sam."

"Okay. I'll tell him."

I told Sam and he didn't seem to be paying any attention at all. Thinking of that bitch Gertie, he was. But luckily he had his uniform. "It's in my duffle bag, checked down at the station."

"What kind of shape is it in?"

"Okay. Just had it cleaned before I took off."

"All right. Have a bath and a shave and look good. Looking smart and clean and neat is very important. Better give me the key to that locker and I'll bring home your uniform tonight." But he wasn't listening to me. Just looking worried. "Sam, you understand what I'm telling you?"

"What? Oh sure. Of course."

"Well?"

"What?"

"The key, you big lug. The key to the locker."

"Oh yeah." He fished into the pockets of his ragged trousers, one pocket after another, and finally among a soiled handkerchief, some matches and other assorted junk he found the key. I warned him again about keeping out of Doug's way and left for the barracks. The key was like a hunk of radium in my money pouch.

All afternoon I was jumpy around the ship, doing stupid things, forgetting what I was doing altogether. Lightson was using me to flash semifore flags to a class he was testing, but I fouled up so badly that he took me off that detail and put me to chipping paint."

I kept away from Smiley, too. The less he knew about what was going on the better. As soon as we were dismissed, I beat it down to the station, picked up Sam's duffle bag and took a streetcar home. I tore up to my room, but no Sam. I took the stairs two at a time and found Ma in the kitchen.

"Where's Sam?"

"Why, he went out. About half an hour ago."

"Jesus Keeryst!"

"Robin!"

"Sorry, Ma."

I knew where he'd gone all right. And that's where I went, as fast as the streetcar could take me over to the east side. As I came to the apartment house I saw two police cars parked in front. One local police, the other a Mountie. A little group of people were standing around the door trying to see in. I pushed my way through.

"What happened?" I asked a big man in a windbreaker.

"Damnedest thing you ever saw. Guy went up to Apartment 301 and started a fight. Threw another guy right down the stairwell and then threw a woman after him. They're both dead."

"Oh no! Did they catch the guy?"

"Sure. He didn't run away or nothing." He nodded his head towards the Mountie's car. "In there."

Sam was in there all right, head down. I didn't go over. I couldn't do anything for him. Nobody could do anything for him.

18

Present Arms

"General salute. Pree-zent arms!"

This order was barked at us by Lightson exactly one hundred and fifty times a day. For now I had the honour of being, along with eleven other hand-picked ratings, in a colour guard.

It came about this way. On Monday morning after prayers and hymn and before we broke up for the day's routine, we didn't fall out as usual, but just stood there at attention wondering what was up now. Then the Old Man came strutting out from the front office, exchanged salutes with Lightson and stood in front of us. He was excited, that was plain.

"All right, men, stand easy!"

We stood easy.

"Exactly two weeks from today, this naval division, His Majesty's Canadian Ship *Porpoise*, will have the singular honour of being inspected by a most important person, the most important personage who has ever visited this ship. Commodore Maynard R. Drake, Commanding Officer, Naval Divisions. He will be here for one day and he will make Commodore's Rounds."

He paused to let this bit of momentous information sink in. But since most of the ratings didn't know a commodore from a coxswain there wasn't much reaction.

"Between now and that date," the Old Man went on, "we are going to work to get ready for the Commodore's visit. Every one must do his part." I half expected him to say, *"Porpoise* expects every man this day to do his duty." But he didn't. "That is all," he said, and marched back to his office.

Then Lightson took over. "I can tell from your reaction, or lack of it, that most of you don't fully appreciate the significance of the Captain's announcement. So I will enlighten you. From now until the Commodore arrives here we are going to work at making this place shipshape. We'll scrub and scrape and varnish and paint and polish and holystone and clean until this entire ship is spotless." He paused and there was still little reaction. Then he went on. "And we are going to drill and march until we are the best drilled and marching ship's company in Canada. I want these men to fall out for a special colour guard. Diespecker, Swanson, Horrichuk." He named off nine more and we fell out.

Later he got the twelve of us together.

"You think you've seen drilling. You think you know how to handle a rifle, but you haven't seen anything. By the time I'm through with you, you twelve will act as one man. Every movement will have exact precision. When you shoulder arms it will be as one man; when you present arms it will be as one man. We have only a short while to work on this and we will work on it all day every day!"

So we were issued webbing and side arms and gaiters so that we looked like the shore patrol, and we began drilling.

Lightson hadn't exaggerated. His purpose was to make non-thinking robots of us, so that when he barked an order it didn't go through the brain but by-passed that organ completely and went straight to our feet or our arms or our hands or whatever part of our anatomy was required to perform the movements.

In the beer parlour I talked it over with Smiley.

"The Old Man is bucking for scrambled eggs on his cap," Smiley informed me. "This inspection by the Commodore means a lot to him. Should hear him in the wardroom explaining to the subbies how officers and gentlemen should act. That damned lecher wouldn't know a gentleman if he saw one."

I was so tired and bored and pissed off with all that marching and presenting arms that I scarcely paid any attention. "And how does he think a gentleman should act?" I asked, but I really didn't give a damn.

"Would you believe they all have to get their hair cut to regulation length? The Old Man's picked out one barber in town and insists they all go to him. He even wants the Number One to shave off his beard, but he doesn't come right out and say so. The Number One knows damned well that beards are pusser. Not moustaches, but beards. But the Old Man will get it off him before Drake comes. You'll see."

"I wonder what all this has got to do with winning the war."

"Fuggall. And he gives them long lectures about manners. He must think that all westerners are plough jockeys who've never seen a silver table setting. He tells them which fork to use, for chrissake."

"Who cares?"

"And he's bound and determined they're going to refurnish the wardroom before the big brass comes. Been belly-achin' about that ever since he got here. But the wardroom committee is holding out. These guys are still so close to the Depression they can't spend money on anything. But he'll get his way, you'll see."

"He'd better hurry up."

"Won't take long. He's got the new furniture all picked out." Smiley took a big swallow of his beer. "Oh yeah, there's going to be a wardroom dinner this Saturday. Sort of a warm-up for the big one we'll have when the Commodore gets here. How would you like to help me?"

"Well . . ."

"All the free booze you can drink - within limits, of course."

"The way I feel there are no limits. I'm telling you, if Lightson keeps me off the next draft, I'll cut him up in pieces and flush him down the head."

"Yeah? Well, you keep your hands off Lightson. All he wants is to get you mad enough to hit him. And then will you be in it."

"I can't guarantee what I'll do if I'm not on that draft. The list'll be posted just after the Commodore's visit - or maybe during. Jees, the war'll be over before I ever get a crack at it."

"Never mind. Can I count on you for the wardroom dinner?"

"Oh sure. What the hell."

And so, as they say, the days went by. Poor old HMCS *Porpoise* was having her hide and insides gone over completely. Gallons of paint, gallons of varnish, gallons of metal polish were applied. In fact the old tub was mostly paint and varnish. I had the funny feeling there was nothing at all underneath all that makeup. Just rotting wood and masonry with a glossy exterior. Take away the gloss and the edifice would crumble. I would fantasize as I marched up and down swinging my rifle hither and thither - it had all become so automatic to me I could think of other things and still do it perfectly - of stealing some cordite from stores and blowing the place up. But I could never think of a time when only the Old Man and Lightson would be aboard, and I didn't want to hurt anyone else.

Then one evening when I was on duty the quartermaster found me where I was holystoning the deck of the recreation room.

"There's a girl on the quarterdeck wants to see you, Dink."

A girl! Patricia? Maybe she'd forgiven me after all. Since the disastrous incident of the dinner table I hadn't spoken to her. How could I? What could I say? Look, I was carrying those french safes because they'd been issued to me and I had forgotten about them and they just happened to pop out. Oh yeah? Sure. Tell that to your old man. Think I was born yesterday?

So I hadn't even phoned her to apologize. I was going to, but Smiley was dead against it. "She's waiting for you to phone and try to apologize," he explained, "so that she can savour the moment. Women love men most when they are apologizing, when they've been naughty and require forgiveness, when they are contrite, humble, begging. What great priests they'd make, and how they'd enjoy the confessional. 'Forgive me, Mother, for I have sinned.' 'Yes, my son, tell Mother all about it.' Hell, that's why the Catholic Church has held out against women priests. They'd enjoy it too much!" Of course I hadn't believed a word of it, but I hadn't phoned.

Now I found a rag and wiped my hands and tried to make my fatigue clothing look a little neater, but it was no use. As soon as I got through the door I saw that it wasn't Patricia.

This girl. How can I describe her? Beautiful? No, not quite beautiful. Pretty? Yes, but something quite beyond prettiness. Brownish hair, small turned-up nose, clear complexion of a country girl who's consumed more milk than wine. A cute little woollen cap on her hair, a cheap coat with rabbit fur collar, nice legs, tiny feet. And a smile! When she smiled she lit up the world, and normally she smiled a lot.

But she wasn't smiling now. She looked worried, concerned, sad. When I got close she held out her hand and said, "I'm Doreen Jones."

"Jones?"

"Mike's sister."

"Mike's sister! Well, hello. Gosh. Mike. Haven't heard from the old rascal in weeks. He used to write me when he first went away, but I haven't heard for –" I stopped. Tears were gathering at the corners of her eyes. "Hey. Is anything wrong?"

"Mike is dead." She swallowed hard. "I didn't want to tell you like this, but I don't know any other way to tell you and I couldn't just let you –" She had her handkerchief out now and was wiping those blue eyes.

"God, dead! Mike! First Sam. Now Mike. This bloody, rotten war!"

"We just got the word yesterday. A telegram. I got right on the train and came to Wabagoon. I couldn't stay home any longer. Mother – and Dad, too – they're so strange about it." She drew in air through her little nose, hard. "I'm going to join something."

"Look, I've got to know more about this. Can I meet you somewhere and we can talk? I'll be off in half an hour. Have you got a place to stay?"

"I'm at the YWCA on King Street."

"Yeah, I know it. Could I pick you up there later?"

"Yes, yes, of course. I'll be waiting."

She was gone.

All I thought of then was the poem of Rupert Brooke that we memorized in high school. "They are not dead, the soldier and the sailor. Fallen for freedom's sake."

Bullshit. They are dead. Dead and gone. Wasted. Killed for the mistakes of politicians. For the power and hunger and greed and just plain stupidity of others.

I picked up Doreen at the YWCA and took her to the Palace of Sweets, the one restaurant that was open, and we sat down in a padded booth. The place was almost empty, the servicemen preferring the beer parlours.

Doreen dimpled at me across the table. She was a warm, loving girl. "May I have a banana split?" she asked.

"Sure, if that's what you want."

"They're my weakness. The drugstone at home used to make wonderful ones."

"Tell me about home."

"Not much to tell. Two hundred and fifty people. Or there were until ten went to war." Her eyes misted over. She reached for my hand, naturally and lovingly.

"Other brothers and sisters?"

"No. Just Mike and I. He is – was – two years older. We did a lot of things together as teenagers. He sort of protected me." She smiled. "I needed protection. Oh, we went to sports days together. Mike was a great baseball player and I played softball." She held up a left hand with a swollen first knuckle. "Softball. Dad runs the general store in Wannego, or he did before the Depression. Then he lost the business. We were on

174

relief. Mike quit school in Grade Ten. I got my senior matric and wanted to go to Normal School but couldn't afford it. Then the war came." She sighed a heavy sigh.

"What did Mike do before he enlisted?"

"What could he do? Hung around for a while and played pool mostly. Then he went on the bum. Rode the freights to Vancouver. Found nothing and came back. Hung around some more. Played more pool. Sometimes he'd hustle the travelling salesmen who dropped into the poolroom and thought they were pretty good. Mike was good at poker, too, and made a little that way, playing in the hotel all night sometimes. I guess he was a little wild, but he was good and kind and gentle. And oh, I did love him." She was crying again.

Try as I might I couldn't think of anything to say to this broken-hearted girl. The preacher, I know, would have fine words about his great sacrifice and his nobility. And the other townspeople and businessmen who didn't care what happened to him before September 3, 1939. Mike had to die to be appreciated.

"Doreen, what happened to him?"

"Lost at sea. It was his first run. Corvette, escort duty, sunk by a submarine."

I thought of Mike in that North Atlantic water. Cold, cold and lonely, using the tricks they taught us in the YMCA swimming pool to stay afloat, the cold water paralysing him.

She hadn't touched her banana split. The ice cream melted around the banana and the whipped cream broke up into little curdles.

"And you want to join up, too?"

"Oh yes. If they'll take me. Are they recruiting girls?"

"Not yet. But they probably will."

She looked at me. "Why haven't they shipped you out?"

There is was. Mike lost at sea. Me sitting pretty on shore, safe and sound from all alarm. Lucky me.

"It's a long story, too rotten for your tender ears. But I'm going to make the next draft, by God, or there'll be trouble."

She didn't say anything to that. We sat and held hands. I got her to eat something and then took her back to the YWCA.

19

Love,
Thy Magic Spell

The visit of Commodore Maynard R. Drake was the biggest thing that had happened aboard HMCS *Porpoise* since the beginning of the war. Practically all training was suspended as all hands were put to work at scraping, painting, scrubbing, or polishing. With everybody wearing fatigue overalls the old place looked more like the garage it had formerly been than a ship in His Majesty's Canadian Navy. We were going to put on a good show or Lieutenant Commander Austin Featherby would know the reason why.

Lightson was a man possessed. It was as though everything he'd ever wanted or believed in had all come down to one grand event, the colour guard. He worked harder than we did, strutting up and down in front of us, hard heels clicking on the concrete deck, chest out, head erect, eyes blazing with the kind of fervour that must have blazed in the eyes of Genghis Khan. His voice had almost gone, sounding like an old wood rasp on a piece of maple.

"One footstep! One footstep! That's what I want to hear; not two or six or twelve. Your feet come down as one foot, your arms move as one arm, your rifle butts hit the deck as one rifle butt! Understand?"

Over and over again he harangued us, back and forth, back and forth he marched us. If marching was going to sink subs we were a cinch to break the Allied record. And as the time approached for the big moment, he became absolutely maniacal.

"If one of you fouls up, just one, I can't even imagine what will happen to you!" It seemed that he was glaring right at me. Why, I wondered, had he chosen me for this duty? Me with my snafu record. If I'd been him I'd have had nothing to do with the likes of me. But actually I was feeling pretty good. All the marching and weapon drill had made a non-feeling automaton of me. I found that I could perform the movements and still think of Doreen.

Ah, Doreen. Friday night before the big day I took her to the Orpheum Theatre to see a movie, starring Errol Flynn as a dashing war hero who knocked hell out of the Germans single handed. While Doreen ogled dashing Errol I ogled her and the more I ogled the more excited I got. So, when Errol took the girl into his arms in one of those great embraces the movies used to be so good at, I reached an arm over Doreen's shoulder and gave it a squeeze. She snuggled over against me, and although I wasn't sure whether the snuggle was for me or for Errol, it set my pulse to racing and my trousers to bulging.

Afterwards, in the Palace of Sweets, she paused halfway through her banana split and gave me a long look.

"What's the matter, Robin?" she asked. "You look, well, kind of funny."

"Huh? Oh. I'm okay. Great, in fact."

"I'm sure you'll be on the next draft. They can't keep you here any longer surely."

"Draft? Oh yeah, draft. Don't worry, I'll be on it. But how about you? How are you getting along?"

"Well, they're not recruiting any girls right now, so I'm just waiting. But I got a job – as a waitress – at the King Richard dining room. Funny how easy it is to get jobs now."

"Doesn't sound like much of a job."

"Oh, it's not so bad. The dining room is a pretty posh place and it's mostly air force and army and navy officers and their wives or dates. They've all got lots of money. One man gave me a dollar tip! That's more than I earned for a whole day's work back home in the dairy."

"Yeah, times have changed."

And they sure had changed for me. Instead of fretting about the slings and arrows of Lightson and the colour guard, here I was thinking only of this girl across the table from me.

Call it love, call it chemistry, call it lust, call it what you like, the fact is I was smit. Every smile, every gesture, every cute little tilt of the head sent electric sparks clear through me. Talk about climbing the highest mountain or swimming the deepest sea, that's nothing. I was like a bull moose in rut. If Lightson or the Old Man or even Commodore What's-his-name himself had stood in my way I'd have killed him.

Of course I can't remember exactly all the wild things I said to her, but I can remember that she didn't seem alarmed or surprised at any of them. I do remember that I blurted out, "Hey, will you come to the dance with me? The draft dance? It's a week from Monday."

And she said, "I'd love to."

And what about Patricia? I hear you ask. Weren't you just as keen for that little mouse? Didn't you get all hot and bothered when you were near her? What kind of fickle little crumb were you, anyway?

Yeah, yeah, but this was different. I know, I know, everybody says that, but this *was* different.

Then came the actual day of the Commodore's Rounds. Excitement had built up during the week to an almost unbelievable pitch. Everything was in order. The sick bay shone as it had never shone. Nothing out of place. I'm sure that if any rating had come down with pneumonia the Old Man would have let him die rather than bring any disorder into that immaculate sick bay. The entire ship gleamed and glistened like a bride awaiting her groom.

And the groom came. He arrived by train and was to be picked up by the longest, most chrome-bedecked limousine in the city, a Packard straight-eight, loaned for the occasion by the Rest Easy Funeral Home. ("Here you can be sure your dear ones are treated as they deserve.")

178

Everyone had been instructed a dozen times just where to stand and what to do. The car would pull up to the side door--quarterdeck - and on that deck all of the officers would be lined up with shoes gleaming as they had never gleamed before. That was on one side. On the other side was the colour guard, ready to present arms the moment the Commodore stepped aboard. The entire ship's company was mustered on the parade deck, waiting to be inspected.

We'd all been honed to a fine edge. Every nerve stretched like a violin string. We couldn't have been more tense awaiting the second coming.

Then a little rustle went through the assemblage like wind gently rustling the leaves, and somebody whispered, "He's here." Outside on the street we heard muffled voices. Then the boatswain's pipe sounded loud and clear, and he stepped up to where the Captain stood slightly apart from his officers, saluted briskly and announced in a loud, clear voice:

"Sir, the Commodore's barge is alongside."

That did it. I don't know if it was the strain I'd been under or whether those words somehow epitomized the absurdity of the situation, of the "ship," of the stupid war itself, but whatever the reason it hit me like a sledgehammer and I burst out into completely uncontrolled laughter.

I'd had this happen before. I'd laughed in church, at weddings, at funerals. I can't understand why, but pomp and ritual always strike me as hilarious. But on no occasion had my untoward laughter been so disastrous as now.

It seemed to break the tension of the previous two weeks of brain-washing. Laughter spread along the first row of the colour guard like fire along a fuse. When Lightson barked, "Colour Guard, Present Arms!", the result was chaos. Guns were pointing in every direction, twirling crazily, my own flying out of my hands and clattering to the cement floor.

Commodore Drake, who had got out of his barge and marched onto the quarterdeck to the strains of the bosun's pipe, carefully practised for weeks, stopped and stared in bewilderment at the giggling mass of incompetents before him. It was one of those situations that nothing could mitigate. Complete and unadulterated disaster.

20

Showdown

The rest of that day was bad. Commodore Drake made his rounds with appropriate pomp and ceremony. Lightson, grim-lipped and worried, made damned sure that I was well out of range of anything or anybody that I could foul up. Now and then I caught him looking at me speculatively as though trying to think what punishment could possibly suit my heinous crime.

At Stand Easy I stood alone and miserable. Nobody wanted to come near me. I was contaminated. Smiley, my one true friend, was busy in the wardroom, standing by for what-ever the Commodore might require. Even Binns left me alone.

In my mind I was formulating a desperate plan. If I were left off that draft list again I'd run away. Like a child leaving parents who can't understand him, I'd take off, change my name, get some forged papers somewhere and join, if not the Foreign Legion, at least the Canadian Army. I'd go overseas and volunteer for the most hazardous assignments and get killed. Then they'd be sorry.

This lovely bit of self-pity was interrupted by Sub-Lieute-nant (Special Branch) Dydell who came up to where I was sitting slumped on a chair and stood in front of me. I got up and started to salute but he waved it away.

"You look rotten, Dink," he said.

"I feel rotten, sir. What's happening in the wardroom?"

"Oh the usual. Commodore Drake is going over some of his First War experiences and the rest are sitting around listening politely." He rubbed his chin. "But I wanted to talk to you about something else."

"Something else?" What else could there be?

"Well, I was wondering if perhaps you'd like to put in for officer's training."

"Me?"

"Yes. Your marks have been good and your M test score is exceptional."

I had a very strong feeling in my right leg as though it were being pulled. But, no, this wasn't Schoolie's style. He was dead serious.

"I can give you a strong recommendation," he said, "and I know Binns will, too, and Number One."

"But, sir, I'm the greatest foul-up that's hit the navy since King Alfred established it! Ask anybody. If the Germans knew about me they'd put me on their payroll."

"As a rating, yes, but I think you'd make a dashed good officer."

"You do? Okay. Suppose I did get by the selection board, what would happen then?"

"Why, you'd go to Cornwallis for officer's training."

"More training! Nothing doing. I've had all this kind of training I can take. I want to get to sea!"

He looked very uncomfortable and sad then. "But what if you aren't on the draft list?"

Had to be careful here. No point in blabbing my plans to an officer. "Oh I'll think of something."

"What?"

"I don't know. But I know damned well I'm not hanging around this dump for another six weeks taking all that guff from Lightson!" Damn, I'd done it.

Schoolie started to say something and then thought better of it and turned on his heel and left. I didn't like the purposeful expression on his face. Probably going straight to the Captain to report. Officers!

Just before we were dismissed the draft list went up. My name wasn't on it.

I stormed into Lightson's office, shouting, "My name isn't on the draft list!"

He was seated at his orderly desk with an open copy of King's Regulations and Admiralty Instructions in front of him. He looked up and smiled.

"I seem to have heard that line before. I know your name isn't on the draft list, Dees-pecker. For a very good reason. How could I throw the book - this book - at you if you weren't here?"

"I can't stay in this hole another six weeks!"

"You may stay a lot longer than that."

"You can't do it! I'll go over the hill!"

"That would be the navy's gain. And come to think of it, probably save a few lives. But you won't do it." His thin lips grew taut. "You're too yellow. No, you'll stay right here. The Old Man has plans for you. After all, he figures you fouled up his other plans to become a full commander." He went back to reading K.R. and A.I.

I stood there looking at him, so mad I knew that if I tried to speak or even move I'd completely lose control. That's what Lightson wanted. The one quick act that would precipitate me into a court martial. The moment passed and I fled from the office.

Later Smiley found me skulking in a corner alone.

"Hey, Dink," he said.

"Go away."

"What?"

"I can't talk. I just can't talk."

"No, wait. Cool it, Dink. I want to show you something."

"Stuff it."

"Okay." He took a piece of paper neatly folded from his inside pocket. "I just thought you might be interested."

"In what?"

"Well, it just goes to show you can't tell about people."

"What people?"

"Take the Schoolie now. I never would have figured him for a sea lawyer. No, I wouldn't."

"Smiley, for Pete's sake."

"But, like he says, K.R. and A.I. was written for the protection of ratings, too."

"What in hell are you talking about?"

"K.R. and A.I. The Schoolie's been studying it. And it says in there that any rating can request to see the senior officer aboard, if he puts his request in writing, as laid down in K.R. and A.I."

"The senior officer?"

"Not the Old Man. The senior officer aboard right now is Commodore Maynard R. Drake."

"So?"

"So what have you got to lose? Schoolie typed this out all legal. All it needs is your signature. You sign it and I'll take it to Drake myself. He's in the wardroom right now, alone, having a little rest."

"Jees, Smiley. You think it might work?"

"As I say, what have you got to lose?"

So I signed the paper and almost right away I was summoned to the Presence. Commodore Drake was a short man with an intelligent face. He was sitting in the Old Man's office at the Old Man's desk, showing an awful lot of gold braid.

I stood in front of him. He looked at me shrewdly.

"Where did you get the idea for this request?"

"I'd rather not say, sir."

"All right. It's most unusual. In fact, the first time I've ever received such a request. All right. What is your complaint?"

So I told him. Once I got started it came out like water from a drainpipe, gushing, with little or no coherence. When I finished, Drake just sat there looking at me.

Then. "You realize, of course, that your punishments were justified."

"Yes, sir. I'm not complaining about that."

"Then what is it you want?"

"To get out of here, sir. To go to sea! I've learned everything they have to teach me here. I don't even take classes any more. I just help teach and do other joe jobs around the place. It's a terrible waste. Now I've been left off the draft list again!"

He opened a folder that lay on the desk in front of him. "I know about your grades. They're very good. High M Test score." He pursed his lips. "Do you think you could get along with your superiors at sea?"

"I know I could, sir. Before I joined the navy I never got into trouble with anyone. Not at school. Not anywhere. I just, well, sort of got off on the wrong foot here."

"Yes, you did." He thumbed through the folder again. "It happens." He wasn't talking to me, but to himself. "Yes, it happens." Then he looked at me.

"Diespecker, don't get the wrong idea. Everything that's happened to you here was largely your own doing. The navy is a big organization, bigger than you, bigger than I. The rules of the navy have been worked out over many years, and they work. Remember that, they work." Oh shit, here it comes again. "The navy doesn't change to suit you, or me, or anybody else. There are thousands of men and dozens of ships." But I wasn't listening any more. The same old song, the same old tune, just a different singer. Smiley and his bloody ideas. Naval officers! They're all the same. Stick together. He finished and told me I was dismissed.

Smiley was waiting for me when I came out of the office.

"How did it go, Dink?"

"Same old guff."

"Well, I tried."

"Yeah, thanks."

"What are you going to do?"

"I'm leaving here. First weekend leave I get, if I ever get one, I'm cutting out. Be four days before they start looking for me and by that time I'll be in the army. Under a different name."

"You'll never get away with it."

"Why not? There's a guy here right now who deserted from the army in Toronto. Hell, they don't even ask for a birth certificate. I can easily get some more papers."

"That's a lot of bull, Dink, and you know it."

"Got a better idea?"

"Naw. I used up the only good one I got. Hey, what the hell?" He pointed across the deck to the bulletin board where the draft list was posted.

Lightson's bumboy was taking the list down. He walked into Lightson's office with it and in a minute came back out again and posted it up. Smiley and I were across there like a couple of torpedoes. And there at the bottom of the list a name had been added.

Diespecker, R.E.F.

"That's you!" Smiley shouted. "It worked! There is some justice after all."

I just stood there staring numbly. Now that it had happened I couldn't respond.

"Dink, we're getting out of here! Both of us! Next week we'll be in St. Hyacinthe and then, of boy. Hey, what a draft party this is going to be!"

That did it. The draft party. Yeah, the draft party!

21

And Away We Go

In many of the books I used to cart home from the Wabagoon Public Library when I was a kid, each chapter would begin with a list of "in-whiches." For instance, "Chapter Eight . . . in which Sir Roger goes on a journey and makes a strange discovery, etc." So I'm doing the same with this chapter, in which:

- I get my love life more or less straightened out, more or less permanently.
- C.P.O. Lightson shows his true colours.
- The Old Man gets what he deserves.
- I make a strange discovery and a big decision.
- Schoolie gets drunk again.
- I'm caught with my pants down.

The second draft party was much the same as the first one, except in this one I was a participant instead of a lookout for dry-land subs. The first thing I learned at this party was that Doreen was a wonderful dancer. Light as a feather and full of rhythm. I've never been a really good dancer and when I'm with a partner who is the least bit wooden I tend to walk all over her feet. But Doreen now, no matter where I went or what step I assayed, she was right there with me all the way. In no time I was cavorting about the deck like Fred Astaire with Ginger Rogers in his arms. It was wonderful, it was grand, it was heavenly.

The second thing I noticed was that Patricia was there with the Old Man. Imagine that! After being chased through the paths of the university grounds and only being saved from "a fate worse than death" by my timely interference, here she was at the dance with that old decrepit wolf. Could it be that, like Svengali, he had hypnotized the dear girl so that he could have his wicked way with her? No, she didn't seem the least under a hypnotic spell. Rather, she was very much alive and enjoying herself.

At first I tried to avoid her, feeling guilty as I did, but I soon quit that. When we danced close to them I smiled and said, "Hi," but she didn't seem to notice me.

I didn't really care either. The presence of Doreen in my arms, so close and warm and cuddly, was doing drastic things to me. And when she looked up at me and smiled I just naturally bent down and kissed her. And she kissed me back, hard.

There is no doubt that during a long lifetime there are events and happenings of such great import that your life is never the same again. That kiss was one of those. With it all my natural reserve and caution and shyness disappeared. All my ambitions and desires in life now centred on one thing - kissing that delicious mouth. And so I manoeuvred her back through the side door of the recreation room and out into the dark end of the drill hall and proceeded to kiss her again and again and again and again.

It wasn't that I had carnal thoughts, it was just that I had no thoughts at all. Lust had completely taken over. The same thing had happened to Doreen. We were goners.

And then as fate would have it, we found ourselves at the door of Lightson's little office and that door was open and there was nobody inside but there was a nice comfortable couch. Well, when you put all those conditions together and us being in the state we were, there is only one thing that can happen. We slipped inside and when we closed the door it was pitch dark, which was good because, as Shakespeare has said, "Lust and light are deadly enemies."

In the movies in those days, as opposed to the movies of to-day, the director had a device for thwarting the moral code of the Hays office. When the man and woman were ready for the hot encounter, the camera wandered away to a flower or a tree or a lake or a moon and left the rest to the imagination of the audience. So let it be with this camera.

I have no idea how long we were there in the dark. Away off I could hear the strains of the orchestra playing a song, one of the lines of which ends with the words, "You take me to paradise."

And just at that moment the door opened and the light went on and there was Lightson standing in the doorway of his office observing a most interesting tableau on his couch. I came back from paradise in one hell of a rush. I looked up at him and there we were face to face, and I knew my goose was cooked.

No draft for me, I knew. Probably a court martial and drummed out of the service, maybe even the cat-o-nine-tails. But that just shows I had a lot to learn about navy ways and navy men. The look of complete amazement on Lightson's face was replaced by a smile, a rather sardonic smile.

"Excuse me," he said and shut the door.

And later, when I passed him on the dance floor with a gorgeous brunette in his arms, he winked at me as though we shared some delicious secret, which, come to think of it, we did.

I felt then, as I have thought ever since, that from the time I met Doreen my bad luck changed. I changed. I quit do-ing the bungling, stupid things I'd been noted for. I also became a man of action. I was determined to get married that very night. I had found the girl I wanted and wasn't going to take any chances on losing her. Suddenly I wasn't so sure I wanted to go on that draft, all I could think of was making love to Doreen every hour on the hour.

I left Doreen with a friend and began rushing about trying to find somebody who could help us get married before eleven o'clock. Since it was already ten, I obviously had to work fast. There was no chaplain aboard, and so I sought out Smiley.

During a brief respite from his wardroom duties, I found him dancing with a girl he'd had his eye on for some time. He wasn't happy about the interruption.

"Dink, what the hell do you want?"

"Can I talk to you for a minute? It's important."

"So is what I'm doing."

"This is more important. Won't take long."

I dragged him off to a corner and told him I wanted to get married.

"Fine," he said. "Now can I go?"

"I mean tonight."

"Impossible. Besides, remember what they say: 'Marry in haste, repent at leisure.' "

"Never mind that crap. This is different."

"That's what Sam said." And then noting the look in my eye he quickly added, "I know Doreen isn't anything like Gertie. But it's impossible."

Next I sought out Binns and found him sitting on a chesterfield in the recreation room sipping a coke and talking to a nice English woman whom he introduced as his wife.

"Harry, I want to get married."

He glanced sideways at his wife. "Marriage is a fine thing for a young lad. Settles him down."

"I mean right now."

"Before you go?"

"Is it possible, Harry? Is there any way?"

"No. No time, lad. You'll have to wait for your first leave."

No help there. Before I could dash off to get help elsewhere, Harry continued. "You know, I'm going to miss this old place. It's not much. Not shipshape as they say, but I've enjoyed myself. Made some good friends, too. The Captain has helped me a lot."

"The Old Man? Surely you jest."

"No, indeed I don't. You've got to remember, lad, that you see this ship entirely from your own point of view and you judge it by how you got along. But he's got the responsibility for the whole crew, and a lot more. He doesn't pick on you. You're just a nuisance to him. I dare say he's glad you're going."

"Maybe he can help."

"Can't do any harm to try."

I found the Old Man talking to a group of leading hands and asked permission to speak to him. He listened to my story and, instead of chewing me out, smiled a big, friendly smile.

"Appreciate how you feel, Diespecker. Feel kind of that way myself tonight. But it's out of the question. Naval rules don't permit it, even if there were time. Besides, a little separation might be good for you right now."

"But, sir."

"One more thing, Diespecker. You are a very cocky young man. Very critical in your estimates of people. I think it may come from living out here on the prairies. You seem to have a chip on your shoulder all the time. But you'll get along. You're smart. Maybe you have learned something after all." Then, by Gawd, he actually patted me on the shoulder. "Good luck, Diespecker."

He was right. I had learned something aboard *Porpoise*, but not exactly what he thought I'd learned.

So I went back to Doreen and rescued her from the arms of a tall, dark sailor with whom she was dancing and, I thought, enjoying it too much.

"Look," I said. "We can't get married tonight."

"Whom were you thinking of marrying?" she asked in bewilderment.

"Why you, of course."

"I don't remember you asking me."

"What! Well, I thought. . . . Hey, I'm nuts about you. Will you marry me?"

"Why, yes. I think I'd be glad to."

"Great! Marvellous! We're engaged. Wow! Look, I'll get you an engagement ring soon as I get a chance and we can get married when I get leave. Wow!"

So much for the impetuousness of youth. The crazy wild extravagant plans. But I'd give anything for that moment again. To feel that way.

I went to spread the news to the people on board whom I cared about. Smiley and Binns and Schoolie, and we got pretty drunk together, I remember. Man, it was fine.

And then finally we lined up like a bunch of drunken sailors, which we were, and the Captain made his speech and we marched down Regal Avenue singing "Roll Along, Wavy Navy" with our girls hanging on our arms; and we got aboard the train and continued the party until our booze was all gone and then we fell into our bunks and the train chugged and shunted and banged its way east, away from the prairies and away from the life we'd known since we were born, and into a new chapter in which: